Symphonic Bridges

Marek Stefanowicz

(Maste)

Copyright © 2009 Marek Stefanowicz

All rights reserved.

ISBN: 10: 1461184169
ISBN-13: 978-1461184164

Lean out of the window,
Goldenhair,
I hear you singing
A merry air.
My book was closed,
I read no more,
Watching the fire dance
On the floor.
I have left my book,
I have left my room,
For I heard you singing
Through the gloom.
Singing and singing
A merry air,
Lean out of the window,
Goldenhair.

James Joyce (*Chamber Music,* 1907)
Syd Barrett (*The Madcap Laughs,* 1974)

Foreword

I wholeheartedly love this book. I have read thousands of books, literally thousands – including hundreds upon hundreds of New Age, spiritual, and "self-help" books. As a journalist I have interviewed a host of so-called 'gurus' and experts. I have even, for my egotistical sins, written over twenty books on wellbeing and spirituality myself. So why is it that this one book, in particular, touches me so deeply?

It's something I've been puzzling since I first read *Symphonic Bridges*. It isn't always easy; in fact it can be downright perplexing. A lot of people run flinching from it, saying it's 'self-indulgent' or 'crazy'. I can sort of understand those reactions. It isn't a 'safe' book; it doesn't play by the standard rules; it doesn't do what it's told. That's partly what delights me about it. The puritanical editor in my head yearns to grapple with it; to cut and paste and add and splice; to wrestle and reduce. My soul taps the editor gently on her stiff-as-a-board shoulder and says, 'That's ego talking again; leave it be.'

It's more than that though. Firstly I really do think/feel Marek has distilled spiritual thought and philosophy down to its pure essence. You can drive yourself crazy going round in circles, reading, researching, trying to understand, trying to be clever, making it all very complicated. But, at heart, spiritual truth is probably very *very* simple. Do you want to live a more balanced, spiritual life? Everything you need is here, pretty much. It set me back on the right path and, when I'm feeling very dramatic, I say it saved my life. Do I agree with it 100 percent? Not yet. *smile*

But Marek won't tell you what to do. And that – I think – is why I *really* love this book so much. He wraps the spiritual stuff up in the fabric of his own life, splicing it into a sort of apologetic autobiography. In many ways it reads like a love story: about divine Love mirrored in the very human love he feels for his wife and soul-mate (a lovely and loving microcosm of the macrocosm).

He tells you what he believes, what he does, and what he hopes he will get out of it. But he never ever says "*you* must do this". That is my beef with so many of the New Age gurus and self-professed Masters: they're bossy and they're big-headed. They don't seem to realise that everyone has to find his or her own way; that you can lead the proverbial horse to water but us horses can be bloody-minded. And there is no one pure way. Ultimately we have to choose for ourselves – we can control our bodies, our minds, our destiny – or we can float. No judgement if you float...floating is fine.

It's not a worthy book either and, dear God, do I loathe worthiness. There is humour and fun and lightheartedness mixed with sadness and frustration and anger (mainly directed at himself). It's human, so human.

Finally, if you love language, surely you have to smile at the way he plays with words? And (okay, so that wasn't the final finally) if you have a mystic's soul, doesn't that soul soar when it peeks over ego's shoulder and reads something like:
"The true nature of Time and Space cannot be known. It can only be heard. Do you see?"

Ah, what else can I say? I can't persuade you; you have to decide for yourself. Personally, I reckon it's got the makings of a cult spiritual classic. But what do I know? Okay, enough of my bullshit. Make up your own mind (just listen to soul as well, eh?)

2011

Jane Alexander (author of such bestsellers as *Spirit of the Home: How to Make Your Home a Sanctuary*, *Sacred Rituals at Home*, *The Detox Plan: For Body Mind and Spirit*, *The Energy Secret: Practical Ways to Energise Every Aspect of Your Life*, *The Five Minute Healer: A Busy Person's Guide to Vitality and Energy All Day, Every Day*, *Mind, Body,* Spirit, *Live Well: The Ayurvedic Way to Health and Inner Bliss*, *The Weekend Healer: Essential Home Programmes to Refresh Body, Mind and Spirit*, *Spirit of the Living Room*, *Spirit of the Kitchen*, *Spirit of the Bedroom*, *Spirit of the Nursery*, *Samael* and *Tanit*)

Black deep lake waters
A thought shines from the bottom
Another one dives

Chapter 1

Opening Passages

Where do i start? (Where does 'i' start?) Here and now, of(f) course. Somewhere in the middle. Of nowhere? Somewhen in the middle. Of nowhen? I wonder ('i' wanders)...

When i am writing this, am i not thinking of those who might be reading it? And when i am reading this, do i not have a feeling that it is just about my ego and its will to wallow in miserable selfishness? And to endear others to itself? What do i expect? (What does 'i' expect?)

When exactly did my conscious mind separate itself from the rest of my being? How real has that obvious projection become? Can a thought be creative enough to authenticate an illusion eventually?

*

As a matter of fact, everything is One. And One is everything. Spirit pervades all elements in all dimension, including physical body. And brain, mind's home, is a body part. The deep structure of all we can imagine (and all we cannot) is White Light Wave. The only difference between a thought and a stone is the frequency rate.

The division of a human being into Spirit, mind and body is a concept developed by conscious mind. Surface mind. Ego. And when we eat only from the tree of knowledge of good and evil for years, the division becomes real. To us. That's a subjective or individual truth.

In order to understand objective or universal truths and to see through the verisimilitude, we must learn how to eat from Tree of Life. (A)gain. Surface mind needs to quiet down and listen to vibrations of the deep structure. To hear White Light Wave.

*

Enlightened surface mind does not speculate about such abstract issues as Infinity. The true nature of Time and Space cannot be known. It can only be heard. Do you see?

Eternity lasts only for a moment. And every second is eternal. All that is must be coherent, by principle and par excellence. But scientists will al(l)ways know only as much as their instruments can measure.

While it comes from Heart...

*

Human brain is a universe. So is the inside of a quark. Vast, empty space flashed across with impulses travelling with the speed of light in all possible (and impossible) directions. Many at a time. Conscious (surface) mind files what it can grasp. In its combined library and laboratory, it analyses what has been filed. Using words as tools. Mostly inefficient means of conveying ideas.

Subconscious (deep) mind not only secures proper functioning of all organs and systems of physical body but it also stores information on our genetic and contextual conditioning, and takes decisions based on such data. Surface mind will never know what deep mind is doing. But it can hear it. If it listens carefully.

Conscious choices are only like drops of water on the subconscious decision-making rock. Yet, little by little can do the trick. If surface mind becomes enlightened, it will understand more than just itself. The petty 'i am' it used to wake up with every morning will not drown out the divine 'I AM' anymore. I AM soaring in the air. I AM pervading all that is.

*

Have i been (has my 'i' been) caressed by a few rays of Absolute then? Why do i hope this urge to write down something that has been gathering for years is any meaningful? Don't i just want to set my thoughts and feelings in order to (re)establish sanity? Or to try to save this one life's experience from oblivion?

If meant for better self-understanding, my narration has to be 100% personal. On a 'Soul-to-Soul' basis. So, I must let all these words pop up. As there are more. Pushed from behind by many feelings, thoughts and ideas. Swelling. Ready to leap out. Like foaming sperms after too long a suppression.

Those who know me wouldn't believe it. I usually stammer a sentence or two every other day. And now i am litera(ri)lly throwing them up. Is this whole writing thingy meant to be a process of intellectual and spiritual cleansing then?

Am i writing that i am writing? Sure! Why not? Who can prevent me from breaking all possible rules in this... anti-book?

*

This text seems a living organism to me. Sometimes growing on its own. Coming from Heart...

No, not the 'big pump'. Not the muscle in the left side of the chest. But the major centre of energy body. Anahata Chakra, symbolized with twelve-petal lotus. Humming 'YAM-NAMAHA'. Pulsating with 'KLIM' sound. Can you hear it? This is the actual Seat of the Soul. Home of Love. Yellow-pink-blue flame burning right in the middle of the chest. Do you see?

No? Well... So far no good then. Apparently, starting somewhere in the middle (of nowhere) and somewhen in the middle (of nowhen) doesn't work. And if i went on describing the present context, i would never get to the point. So, i'd better start from the beginning...

*

Chapter 2

Beginning

I can see two giant shadows on the wall. Trembling. Moving gently. I can hear soothing sounds. The two magical figures are whispering Love and Devotion. My guardians. Caring.

The world is just lights and shades. Glowing silhouettes and comforting voices. First glimpses of awaking consciousness. All so mysterious and full of ephemeral promises.

It's alright now but I still remember being forced out of warm waters of the original home, and deprived of the reassuring regularity of heartbeat echoing in the pleasant twilight right above my head. Then only bright light and strange noises... And fear...

*

Some nine months before... Once upon a time, many dimensions from here and now, in Domain of Absolute, a teeny-weeny fragment of a monstrously-sized Sphere of White Light (hereinafter and thereoutbefore referred to as Centre of Pure, Unconditional and Everlasting Love) chose to taste some relativity in physical universe.

So, it broke away gracefully, forming a perfect Sphere of White Light. Identical with its prototype but probably billions times smaller. Of(f) course, the difference in size could not be assessed due to the fact that in Domain of Absolute everything is irrelative: immeasurable and incomparable.

Having separated itself from Centre of Pure, Unconditional and Everlasting Love, Sphere of White Light travelled through inter-dimensional channels to dive right into my mother's egg at the very moment it was fertilized with my father's sperm. My parents... Making love on planet Earth... All Universe, Infinite Space, in Its profound majesty, held Its breath for a split second. For me... And Sphere of White Light exploded – 'Big Bang' – blazing to illuminate the whole, newly created microcosm of my being.

*

And this happens all the time. All Time. Spheres of White Light leave Centre of Pure, Unconditional and Everlasting Love, participate in physical dimension, experiencing its relativity, and come back, for reunion and sharing...

Of(f) course, this is only a vision. A metaphor. A simplification. God, in all Her/His aspects (including Time, Space and Pure, Unconditional and Everlasting Love) not only pervades physical universe and all other dimensions but SHE/HE IS (I AM) all dimensions as well. She/He is all that is. Al(l)ways.

And it's not a coincidence that we are conceived at the given Time in the given Space. Physical universe is not based on randomness and chaos. Every single event in our life is an outcome (resultant) of many different forces, which operate from many different directions. So, it may seem to occur out of the blue. But it doesn't. Everything is subject to Law of Cause and Effect. Another aspect of God, Who is Love and... Justice. Every feeling, thought, word, action and situation simultaneously follows a stimulus and triggers a response. Of(f) course, we are unaware of this process. Just as we fail to keep up with the course of performance of our brain when it comes, for instance, to controlling the functions of our nervous or digestive systems.

*

White Light from Centre of Pure, Unconditional and Everlasting Love, often referred to as Soul – is our Divine Potential. While the combination of our parents' karmas valid for the moment of fertilization and the given Time & Space – are our genetic and contextual conditioning respectively.

Soul doesn't choose the environment in which She is to experience relativity of physical dimension. As She originates from Domain of Absolute, She is free from any conditioning. Soul is here just to bless our choices, and to participate in the context. God always says 'Yess'. And all Souls are the same. Just different fragments of Grand Oneness. Subject to nothing.

Physically, we are continuations of our ancestors. Combinations of their genes. And every gene is a genie. An infinite microcosm. Containing karmic information on all past generations. Their choices, individual and collective consciousnesses.

This information has tremendous impact on our being. It conditions our foetal life, birth, behavioural patterns in response to different situations, infant dependence, awakening consciousness, relationships, etc. On top of that, all situations in our present life and decisions taken generate new subconscious thinking patters which determine our future choices.

*

So, why are we here and now? There are too many reasons and circumstances. Most of them come from Higher Levels. From Secret Sources. And one simple surface mind, unless enlightened, cannot grasp Whole Picture. We can never know it. But we can hear it. Do you see?

I believe in Order, Harmony and Universal Justice. We do have free will and we can exercise it in abundance. Yet, we should remember that our choices contribute to overall plots. They intermingle with other forces, including any outcome of decisions taken by others. And thus results of our actions may differ dramatically from our expectations. But it does not mean that Law of Cause and Effect is not working. It is. And it does. Al(l)ways.

Sometimes, one lifespan is not enough to experience Universal Justice in the given plot of events. We come back to physical universe as other fragments of Centre of Pure, Unconditional and Everlasting Love. Our conscious minds can remember nothing from our previous visits here to appreciate (or to curse) Universal Justice. Sometimes we manage to find relevant 'files' in 'cabinets' of subconscious mind – information encoded in our chromosomes. But usually these are just conscious mind's projections.

Ego doesn't like the idea of total disintegration after Soul's leaving physical body. But it dies every time physical body dies.

*

Physical body always follows instructions received from subconscious mind. That's where keys to genetic codes imprinted in every cell are kept, and where most crucial decisions regarding our life are taken. Physical body can never do anything against subconscious mind. All its organs and systems are totally subordinated to the brain. Every failure or disease has its roots in subconscious mind's database. Surface mind is only superficial. And it is not enough to think (to say to ourselves) that we are healthier or happier, while the 'big computer' keeps sending signals contrary to our conscious beliefs. Signals considering past karma (genetic conditioning) or those regarding our present life's experience (contextual conditioning).

Logically speaking, if we could live forever. Mortal mind would just need to surrender to immortal Soul. All hitherto patterns of relativity would be then superseded accordingly: Domain of Absolute would take over. And one would become One. (A)gain. The only problem is conscious mind and its projections of separable identity. Ego will al(l)ways object to replacing 'i am' with 'I AM'.

And maybe Sphere of White Light doesn't have to return to Centre of Pure, Unconditional and Everlasting Love at all. Maybe, eventually, the whole Centre will end up participating in physical dimension.

Maybe we can make mortal mind accept superiority of immortal Soul. It would be like trying not only to understand but also to control our dreams. But if we became true masters of conscious breathing, fasting, meditation, visualisation...

*

Conscious mind quiets down. Hears 'I AM' sound. Soul. God. Pure, Unconditional and Everlasting Love. Conscious mind gives up its 'down-to-earth' business. Surrenders to White Light. Permanently. Subconscious mind can't believe it. Its little brother has stopped talking bullshit at last. Now the whole brain echoes with 'I AM'. White Light is taking over. Rising. Burning down all negativity. Destroying bad patterns. Exposing every single element of physical, mental and emotional processes to unlimited opportunities, rejuvenation, everlasting love and happiness...

Conscious mind finds out, to its utmost amazement, that its identity has not been lost at all. On the contrary, now it has much better contact with its big brother and access to Ultimate Truths. It wakes up in the morning (if it goes to sleep at all, as the two brothers don't have to work in shifts anymore) singing 'I AM'. It is now THE CONSCIOUS MIND. And its 'down-to-earth' business has turned out to be THE DIVINE MISSION – THE HEAVEN-ON-EARTH JOB...

If Soul had a mouth, She would smile broadly. Here and now.

*

Chapter 3

Walking Torches

I know i have probably lost most of prospective readers by now, trying to deal with too many things and skimming only over Ultimate Truths. However, those who are still with me understand that the game of words is hopeless from the start when it comes to such spheres of life as Sphere of the White Light. We all know that Big Answers come in silence. When surface mind quiets down. And listens.

If only Soul could speak... But it just keeps glowing with Her flame of Absolute Love. In some of us, She is so dominated and suppressed by surface mind that She can manifest Herself in nothing more than just a flickering spark. Others are WALKING TORCHES. BURNING BUSHES. Like Jesus Christ and many other Masters of Being.

Jesus teaches us that we can master the elements of Earth – through fasting (one apple a day does keep the doctor away, especially when it's the only meal), Water – until we can walk on its surface, and Fire – to become Walking Torches. He tells us we are all God's children, capable of doing greater things than His miracles. And He resurrected His physical body, for Christ's sake!

*

One thing seems to be certain: if we are to reach high, if we are to become the embodiment of Divinity of our Souls, there is no room for moderation. We must forget what we have heard about the necessity to have our feet firmly fixed on the ground.

Besides, the ground is not stable at all. Beneath the crust and the brittle upper mantle (the lithosphere), the semi-fuel zone (asthenosphere) and the lower mantle – there is boiling zone 'D', where the mantle meets the iron core: white hot fluid metal (5800 degrees Celsius). So, 'how do we sleep while our beds are burning?'

This whole bizarre structure rotates on its axis, with the speed of a spot on the equator reaching 1670 km/h. If we add to this, the dizzying speed of the earth's revolution around the sun: 107280 km/h, we'll see ourselves on a monstrous, breathtaking Ferris wheel, suspended in the infinite space together with other 'mechanisms', similar and different... Countless. This is what conscious living is about: to be aware of the context (as big as we can grasp). Then having our feet firmly fixed on the ground will acquire an entirely different significance.

*

Of course, from a long distance, it all looks as if there is hardly any movement. The large solids of the planets seem to hang majestically in Space. Reflecting the vital lights of their suns. So peaceful... Quiet.. Everything is in order... A graceful dance of the spheres... In slow motion...

To understand Harmony of the universe one must look at it from the right perspective, ignoring drama of an individual being: a helpless and despairing man or a sun spitting out white-hot blinding plasma, to the accompaniment of deafening roars of inconceivably powerful and overlapping explosions, until it burns out completely and becomes a red dwarf.

Relativity applies to Time as well. And thus it's irrelevant if man appeared on planet Earth in course of evolution or through an instant act of God (or some aliens' landing). If we present Time (against Its nature) as a numerical axis, then from the right perspective, the millions of years of revolution or the single moment of creation (or the landing), will be just one and the same dot on the line.

Time passes
Bringing His daughter
Change
Letting Law of Cause and Effect
Apply
God in action
Love

*

Chapter 4

Daydreaming

The two-year-old boy is lying on the floor in the foetal position and picturing himself inside a tiny house, with just one room, one door and one window. Feeling secure. It's nice and warm in here. Peace and quiet. Twilight. He doesn't know that his imagination is taking him back to his mother's womb.

He just keeps lying on the floor and daydreaming that he is lying on the floor in the little house and playing with building blocks: his thoughts. Both conscious and subconscious. At this early stage of awareness the two brothers are still very close to each other. So pure and innocent. So full of White Light.

He looks out of the window. The forest is lit with subtle sunshine. And there is so much going on there. All those plants, birds and animals. But also angels, magicians, unicorns, elves, wood nymphs, fairies, dwarfs... With every 'session', the world outside grows bigger and bigger. Featuring more and more creatures from his mother's fairytales.

*

Now and then the boy leaves the house to join his characters in their adventures. And in real life, he never falls asleep at night without visiting the imaginary world for an episode or two. In all his stories, there is always a mysterious mission to accomplish. A secret to guess. A riddle to solve. Can these 'hide and seek' or 'blind man's buff' games be inspired by Soul?

The boy runs into the living room on a Christmas morning and throws himself under the tree. Where mystery at its glory... Amongst the prevailing scent of the Christmas tree needles... Pure magic... He reaches out... Slow motion... His eyes closed... Time stops... All Universe, Infinite Space, in Its profound majesty, holds Its breath for a split second. For him... So close to Ultimate Truths... Life is a gift... I AM speechless...

When the boy is seven, the little house has another dweller. A girl. His classmate. Long hair. Beautiful, blue eyes. They live there together happily. He gets her out of trouble now and then. Saving her from a nasty satyr or a fierce dragon. He's such a hero. Always brave. Always daring. Aiming at victory. And victory always comes. Then the two platonic lovers gallop away on their wonderful horses towards the sunning set. And not a single night without such stories. For years.

*

One day the boy starts to sense that something is wrong. The gap between his imaginary world and reality grows bigger and bigger. At school, the long-haired doesn't even notice him. And he's no hero. Bullies prove it too often. He finds himself hiding from real world, escaping into his daydreaming, reading or watching TV.

His own imaginary life in the fairyland and lives of characters from books or movies seem much so much nicer than his miserable existence in reality.

He doesn't realize that the split of the two worlds is a result of his mind's growing attachment to physical dimension and its relativity. The more he learns, from his parents, teachers and other sources, about real world's limitations, the weaker becomes his mind's connection with Soul.

Isn't it amazing how knowledge can deprive us of our innocence? A Master of Being can levitate only when She/He plays with the law of gravity. Like a child, whose mind can easily catch fire from BURNING BUSH. For Whom nothing is impossible.

*

Year after year the boy's mind separates itself from Soul more and more. The daydreaming is the only 'bridge'. If his mind weren't so selfish, superficial and boastful of its progress in cognition, he would be able to understand signals coming both from Soul and from all Masters of Being and Angels. But stubborn mind never wants to know that the only solution is its dissolution in Soul. Its total surrender...

The is sensitive and emotional. And owing to intellectual development, his perception of the world around him is fuller. Now he can better define his feelings. Everything is still so fresh. All those beautiful scents, sounds and colours of changing seasons. And grass is so green in May...

His eyes, ears and nostrils are wide open. Sometimes even too wide. His behaviour demonstrates symptoms of manic personality, with euphoria for joy and despair for sadness.

*

The boy doesn't know that there are only two sources of emotions: Soul and mind. Pure, Unconditional, Everlasting Love comes from Heart. All other feelings are generated by brain.

He's a goal-keeper. The position suits his 'i' (as in 'individuality') just fine. So spoilt. Lazy boy. Chooses to be the only player in the team who doesn't have to run about the pitch after the ball. The ball comes to him. And he enjoys kissing the ground after a flying save. The element of Earth.

So, does he find any more 'bridges'? Oh yes. Here's one…

*

Chapter 5

Climbing in Circles

I was five. Hanging down from a hanging frame. A funny steel structure. Used for beating dust out of carpets. There were six of them in our housing estate. Each next to a rubbish tip. Among five-storey blocks of flats. Mine was close to the playground. With a few swings and see-saws, two slides and a sandpit. In winter, the playground became a skating rink...

So, I was hanging down from the hanging frame. With my fingers clenched around the ending corner of the top bar. As I had been doing many times before. There was not much else to do. One TV channel. With two short programmes for kids. Black and white. No PC, VCR, DVD, GB, PS, DS, PSP, mp3, mobile phones... Nothing. Just these two programmes. And books...

Of(f) course, the good side was that i spent a lot of time outdoors. But the world outside was then just like TV: black and white. Mostly turning grey. The whole country was sinking in a political and economic lethargy, dragging down with itself my small, obscure, border town into deeper and deeper stagnation. No wonder i turned to spirituality. The chasm between reality and fantasy was a gaping precipice. I needed those 'bridges'. Badly.

*

Anyway, i was hanging down from the hanging frame, with my fingers clenched around the ending corner of the top bar. As I had been doing many times before...

But on that particular day, i started 'climbing' one of the posts in circles: pulling my knees up the chest and lowering them slowly, in a continuous, systematic, enchanted repetition. My knees going up and down. Up and down. My legs in a bizarre dance in the air. Marking time. Rubbing against the cold steel post of the hanging frame. My mind in a trance. Losing control. I felt i was getting somewhere. The 'climbing' was apparently taking me to the summit of a 'mountain': to the top of my emotion. Where physicality was to meet spirituality...

Finally, i was out of breath. And so was all Universe. Infinite Space. In Its profound majesty. Holding Its breath for a split second. For me... So close to Ultimate Truths... Life was a gift... I AM speechless... My arms started to weaken and i got there. With flashes of White and Golden Light in my head. Turning into yellow-pink-blue flames in my Heart. With waves of warmth sweeping all through my body. Up and down. I was shivering with unbelievable pleasure. I felt blessed and delighted. As if i was licking heavens. So sweet. That was it. My mind faced Soul. Touched Her. And fell apart. Collapsed. Disintegrated. Acknowledging Her superiority. Unfortunately, just for w few seconds. What a shame...

*

My first orgasm. Totally mystical experience. At the age of five. Without erection or ejaculation. Without any sexual connotations whatsoever. Yet it was definitely it. As i found out many years later. By comparison.

When i was twenty i saw another boy using my hanging frame for the same purpose. A representative of next generation of researchers. Obsessed with exploration of 'bridges' between mind and Soul.

However, as the five-year-old alleged discoverer of this amazing phenomenon, and later on, when i indulged in excessive experimentation, several times a day, on the staircase handrail or the door leaf – i considered myself a pioneer.

*

Of(f) course, i was too ashamed to share my new experience with anybody. Even my closest friends. Besides, i must have been afraid that if i shared the secret i would derive less pleasure from the 'climbing in circles',. as i associated the bliss and delight with the sense of mystery.

So, i kept walking over the 'bridge'. A lot. Enjoying another link between reality: domain of my mind and body (which didn't seem that bad any more, by the way), and spirituality: domain of Soul.

Those too brief moments of (re)union were Soul's unintentional (as She is beyond anything, including any intentions) lessons on Absolute. It was my mind's choice to learn to feel Pure, Unconditional and Everlasting Love. And it drank in everything eagerly. With hedonistic abandon...

*

I know that the 'climbing in circles' was more atavistic than metaphysical. We inherit the genetically conditioned desire to pursue the sexual pleasure. Obviously related to the animal-like instinct of survival through reproduction.

Many children, if not all of them, to different extent, even though their 'instruments' are not ready yet – start exercising this instinct very early. Like a pre-season training.

My wife's uncle reports scrupulously, nearly every time we meet, how she used to 'make love' to her bed leg by rubbing her loins against it sensually, when she was five. She denies. Pretends not to remember. My dirty little girl...

*

And how does Richie fit in the concept of the juvenile sexuality? My neighbour. Richie. About two years older. One summer, when i was six and a half, he put up his 'tent'. A blanket, with one side hooked over sharp metal elements protruding from the wall of our block of flats, and the other fastened to the ground with nails. He said he would give us some medical examinations. Girls and boys. My age. More or less.

We were called to enter the 'tent'. One by one. Inside, he told us to get undressed and lie down on the stomach, face down, while he was shining his electric torch on our naked buttocks, stroking them occasionally and patting. Practically slavering over his 'medical' success. Dr Richard. Seeing his 'little patients' in his suspicious 'treatment' room...

Nothing original! At the same time, a few hundred kilometres away, my wife went with her cousin and his male friends for a walk. They descended under a bridge, where she was asked to take off her dress and all underwear. She did it willingly. Looking forward to another adventure. And when the boys found out that she had more holes in her body than they did in theirs. One of them decided to insert a piece of a stick into one of the spare holes. For the sake of mere scientific curiosity. If my mother-in-law hadn't spotted them seconds before the experiment was started... Well... I'm not sure whether i would have bought any story, with the obvious alternative conclusion, as an explanation to how my wife had lost her virginity.

*

Enough of this exhibitionism. So much about kids exercising their atavistic sexuality.

*

Chapter 6

Keep Smiling

The more information the surface mind was fed with, the longer the 'bridges' had to be. The gap was growing...

At school, i felt like a herring in a shoal. Especially, during breaks, when i (as in 'individuality') was carried by the crowd from one classroom to another. Or to the locker room. My early experience of the collective consciousness. We were like one organism, one mind, taking joint decisions and making common choices (regarding directions of our relocation, for instance). If we had come across a shark, many of us would have just followed the others slavishly right into the beast's jaws.

No, we couldn't be herrings. Children should be seen and not heard. But we were heard. A lot. Unlike fish. So, we were more like bees. Buzzing all the time. Every form was a swarm. Flying to and fro. Bumping against other swarms. The hive was bursting.

*

I liked learning. It felt right to know more. To be aware of a growing number of different aspects of the surrounding physicality. To understand better what was going on around me.

I wish i had learnt more about the spiritual side of physics, chemistry, maths, biology, etc. It is a pity that they did not confess that the scientists had been wrong thinking that electrons were the smallest elements of the matter, and that they spread their arms helplessly observing mysterious streaks of light inside a quark under a new, field-ion microscope. Or that even the most powerful telescopes failed to detect any boundaries of the outer space.

It's a shame that we were treated like schools of herrings or swarms of bees, and fed automatically with scientific and religious doctrines. While i (as in 'individuality') expected support and cooperation in my own searching and researching...

*

I was disappointed with the system. I'm still an extreme Liberal. Or even an anarchist. To me, all systems are wrong and unnecessary. I don't need law, as i lack desire to commit any offence. I don't need politics to govern me, or religion to interfere in my communication with God (Who is right inside me in the form of my Soul).

Yet, i am a realist too. I tolerate the systems. As there are many people who live unconsciously. Who, for example, would steal mightily if not their fear of punishment: either legal or religious.

I continued the self-exploration. Soon, I discovered another 'bridge'...

*

'What the fuck do you think you are doing? Not again. Put that bottle away. How old are you? Nine? When did it start? Last year? I know you can't hear me. It must have been last year.

So, You found the key in Your father's suit jacket pocket. You unlocked the drinks cabinet and took a long look at the bottles. They were standing there in an arch-shaped row. Smiling. Inviting. Their necks shining...

'Ratafia'? What an exotic name. And the colour. Something between (deep) purple and black (Sabbath). You unscrewed the top. Poured yourself half a glass. And swallowed quickly. You felt fire in your throat. Then radiating warmth in the stomach. And finally comfort and relaxation.

*

Then you lay down on the floor. But you didn't need the foetus position anymore. And the one-windowed house blurred and started vanishing from your head. Dismantled by the alcohol in Your veins. You were just lying on Your back. Facing the ceiling. And the stars high above. Hoping that all Universe... Infinite Space... In Its profound majesty.... Will hold Its breath for a split second.... For you... So close to Ultimate Truths... Life was a gift... I AM speechless...

You enjoyed the physical comfort very much. The experience was not as profound, not as thorough, not as dramatic, as the culmination of the 'climbing in circles' procedure, but it lasted longer... You liked the new "bridge", didn't you?

But now? How many glasses have you had? Six? And You are reaching for another one? If i were your father... No, what am i saying? Anyway, how come your father hasn't noticed anything yet? Ah yes. I know. You take half a glass from every bottle. Six different bottles one day. Other six on another. It's too little to get drunk. You just enjoy the 'condition' for an hour or two, and when your parents come home from work you are totally sober.

*

Thank God i don't have a drinks cabinet in my house. I haven't been drinking any alcohol for nearly twenty years now. Besides, i don't need to go to work. I (as in 'individuality') have an office at home. And people come to me and bring me the money in exchange for my translation services. As a freelancer, i don't have to win any employers' favour. Nor do i exploit any manpower. So, when my sons come back from school, i'm always there. Waiting. The 'guard' of the house.

And i don't smoke. So they have no chance to conceal any bad habits from me. Do you smoke? Of course, you do. And you are only nine years old. My younger son is now three years older than you...

My dear, dear boy...

*

I think a lot about you these days. Maybe it's the 'mirror syndrome'... Believe me: this is no fucking 'bridge'! This is another delusion. Your mind does not connect with Soul. She has nothing to do with it.

Your mind links up with the nation's karma. Thousands of years of widespread alcoholism. Conditioned by the country's history? Determined by the climate?

But what excuses can we invent in Time of Peace (at least in Europe) and the global warming? That's simple: economy. Unemployment, poverty and the sense of social injustice: don't's versus have's. But do they really long for the communistic 'equality'?. There is al(l)ways a pretext to have a drink...

*

This is a 'bridge' between your mind and the minds of those of your forefathers who had alcoholic tendencies. Their consciousnesses were encoded in your parents' genes to manifest themselves at the opportunity of your searching and researching. Nothing more. Don't try to build up any ideologies in excuse to your weaknesses...

You know what? I'll leave you like this. Do i have a choice? When it occurred to me that i should write about you, i wanted to be more severe. I intended to make this passage mercilessly revealing and condemning. I blamed you and your choices for all my future failures, including many years' abuse of alcohol.

But when i'm looking at you now, i can see just a little kid... Smiling happily... You don't mean anything wrong. You have no idea of any complicated conditioning, multi-layer circumstances, Law of Cause and Effect... You are just so happy that you have found another 'bridge' to walk over. Away from bad moments in your real life...

*

I'm sure many kids started drinking even earlier. And not only those brought up in pathological families. Educated background and living in intellectual circles did not prevent you from playing the 'bottle' game.

I know you can't hear me. This monologue was meant to square with the past. The cleansing function of writing, right? But i just want you to know that... i love you...

Take care kid. I know you will. Most of the time. And keep smiling. For soon you will stop doing it in this... innocent way...

*

...

*

Chapter 7

Lake

'So it wasn't a real "bridge", was it?', She asks sadly.
'And were the other two real?' Tears welling in his eyes...
'If they worked...'
'Yes, but so did the third one!'
'Did it?'
'Wait a minute! Who are you?'
'I'm just another part of you, which appeared in the preceding passage.'
'Split personality?'
'Not necessarily. Just another "lyrical subject", if you like.'
'For dialogues?'
'Too.'
'OK. I agree that without dialogues... So far no good... But this was not meant to be a novel!'
'What was this meant to be?'
'My ego's paeans to itself?'
'Now you're too cruel towards yourself.'
'So you have emerged from the three dots above which stand for my loss for words after I scolded my younger counterpart?'
'No. After you said you loved me. Nice talking to you...'

*

The boy falls for music. 'Bridge' number four. After a few years of searching and researching, he finds what suits him best: HARD ROCK.

Just like alcohol has pulled down his little one-windowed house, the harsh, exploding sounds of Deep Purple, Led Zeppelin, Black Sabbath and Uriah Heep will soon frighten away the subtle fantasies from his imaginary world. Falling asleep with the headphones on his ears every night, how can he hear his beloved crying for help?

And thus the fourth 'bridge', jointly with the third one, have ruined 'bridge' number one... Goodbye daydreaming...

*

Music really makes him fly high. His mind switches off deliberately every time the pulsating rhythm puts it into a trans. Gillan's high-peaked and hoarse vocals. (Ab)so(l)u(te)l(y) persuasive. And Blackmore's virtuoso melodious solos. They reach Soul and make Her dance. This is a good 'bridge'.

The boy starts playing the guitar and composing. Lyrics and singing come later.
He spends hours in his room listening to music and playing the guitar. Sometimes forgetting about food. Unconscious fasting. Another proof he's on the right track.

He gets a 'Forte' tape-recorder for Christmas. He feels the same old excitement again reaching out for it under the Christmas tree. Closed eyes... Slow motion... The smell of the tree needles...

*

Now the boy can record his own songs. Playi̇
instruments. One at a time, of(f) course. And sı̱ı̱ͺ
Ping pong. He's fifteen.

He plays in a few bands. But no good at teamwork.
Totally egocentric.
Encounters other music: Beatles, Stones, Pink Floyd
(especially Syd Barrett), Queen, King Crimson,
Doors, Budgie, Rush, and many, many others.

Soon he finds out that most lyrics of his favourite
pieces of music are disappointing. To say the least.
And thus the songs, as a whole, have become less
attractive. Once again, knowledge has deprived him
of innocent pleasure...

*

'No, I can't do it without you. Where are you? If you
are a part of me you must be somewhere here. Speak
up! Please...'
'Hello.'
'Finally! Where've you been?'
'I'm always here.'
'So why have you remained silent?'
'I only speak when you let me.'
'Who are you?'
'But you know!'
'Do I?'
'...'

'Please help me. I think I've lost it. See the passage
above? It's hopeless. And it's about music! MUSIC!'
'It's not that bad. Besides, since it's music you are
supposed to make it or listen to it, and not to write
or read about it. Relax.'
'If you are what I think you are, why did you decide
to join me in this meaningless undertaking anyway?'
'Don't say that... if this comes from Heart...'

*

We were sitting on a sunlit hill. One May afternoon. Fresh breeze from the nearby lake was fanning our faces. The spruce tree tops on the other shore were swaying gently in a magical dance to their soothing swoosh. And grass was so green...

I, my beautiful wife: Maggie, and my cousin's wife: Betty.... Our son and her daughter were running up and down the hill, chasing each other, laughing... Betty was already packed for tomorrow's journey. She was flying to join her husband in the USA. That was our last time together. Maybe for ever...

We were talking about something. Watching the children. I was thinking about Time, my own childhood, my son's future, a possibility of his meeting Betty's daughter again somewhere... Somewhen...

But I remember that moment so well because of the feeling of a profound peace my Heart was then overflowing with. Peace and joy. Wise Joy.

I have the brightest star
Right in my Heart
Shining with pure White Light
Reaching the skies

I was lost and I was blind
Not seeing most obvious of all
Beautiful vibrations

There's no power over Love
Surrender
And You'll always win

One turn
And a brand new day
Good life
To choose
For ever'

(YouTube: Ma.Ste. Wise Joy)

Happiness or its lack is just our mind's interpretation of reality. Either our pituitary gland (hypophysis) and hypothalamus secrete endorphins in the given situation, or they don't. Sometimes, after two days of fasting, I feel so miserable. The only remedy then is to start thinking of something pleasant. A few moments later, I experience my little 'resurrection'.

*

We are sitting on a sunlit hill. One May afternoon. Fresh breeze from the nearby lake is fanning our faces. The spruce tree tops on the other shore are swaying gently in a magical dance to their soothing swoosh. The spruces look taller than they really are, as they overgrow a cliff, which stretches all along the other shore, and the tops of the trees growing lower meet and intermingle with the branches of those growing higher. And grass is so green...

She has long fair hair and green eyes. She's not my classmate from the little one-windowed house of mine, who had blue eyes. She looks just like my wife. Maggie. When we first met. So fresh. So innocent. She is exuding grace and beauty. Her hair blowing in the breeze. Her eyes sparkling with all stars...

Fresh green
Against clear blue
Sunshine in your hair
Bright atoms in the air
Dance and sing
The same old song
And I can't help
Singing it to you
Again

(YouTube: Ma.Ste. Mission Statement)

But She's not my wife. She's glowing with White Light. Blindingly. She's shining like the Sun. Her light is so intense that it makes my body reflect it. I'm Her planet. Mars, of(f) course...

'Why are we here?', She speaks with Maggie's voice. Magic voice. Melodious. Sensual. Soothing...
'Do you like it?' I look around. The surface of Wigry lake is glistening in the sunning set... The fragrances permeating the fresh May air make my nostrils hyperactive. I can smell lush nature, already well-awaken from the winter sleep, bursting with life energy, flourishing abundantly... And grass is so green.
'It's beautiful.' She gives me a radiant smile.
I smile back, slowly getting used to Her trembling beam. 'The place is called Gawrych Ruda, and it's my second home. I used to come here a lot as a child. With my younger sister: Ursula, and our parents. We would go for a walk, play volleyball or badminton. And swim in summertime. As an adult I came here to jog with my Alsatian: Pedro. For fourteen years. And then alone. I still swim here nearly every morning between June and September. And sit at the open fire every fortnight. On Monday.

The first day of my fasting procedure. I feel some kind of a strong attachment to this place. To this lake. As if I had lived here many times before I was born. Is it possible?'
'Hm... Anything is possible. Depending on what you mean when you say "I"...' She keeps smiling, stretches lazily and lays on Her back, facing the clear blue sky, with Her glowing palms underneath Her beaming hair. No, She's definitely not my wife. If She were, we would be making love now...
Regardless of the blinding light. I close my eyes...
'Perhaps, I should erase all the previous passages and start this book from here: on this hill... With you?'
'Ha!'
'What?'
'You said "book".'
'I did, didn't I? Well then... if it were to be a book, it should start here, shouldn't it?'
'Why?'
'To spare the prospective readers all those truisms, banal repetitions, pathetic exhibitionisms, and so on. Do you realize that perhaps right now nobody is reading what we are talking about?'
'But does it really matter?'
'Not any more, I guess...'

*

'Please tell me about Derek and Jack.'
We are swimming in the lake. Naked. Her body is lightening up the darkening waters, which swallowed the red sun minutes ago.

'OK. But first you tell me why you're so shining. Are you an Angel or something?'
'I speak when you let me and I look what you make me.'

'O rly?'. LOL.
'Ye rly!'. LOL.
'Then I'll wipe all the glitter off you with a single stroke of my arm!'
'If you catch me...' And She dives.

*

I follow Her. Evening-diving in the ancient, glacial waters of Wigry lake. It's the third biggest lake in Poland as for the area, but with the longest and most winding shoreline. Actually, 'wigry' means 'winding' in the language of the Yatzwing tribes, who used to live here thousands years ago). The depths of the lake exceed 70 metres.

Its abyss is like a universe. So is the inside of a quark. Vast, empty space flashed across with impulses travelling with the speed of light in all possible (and impossible) directions. Many at a time. Electric lake eels...

'Vast waters
Let me take you in my arms
Your horizon
A fist
And nothing will defeat us
Any more

Immense charm
And force unquenchable
My thought
Your song
And nothing will defeat us
Any more'

(YouTube: Ma.Ste. Węże Morskie Mistrzyni Przypraw)

Lake eels and sea snakes... Magic and Divine Potential... Another 'bridge'... By the water...

Pillar of Fire (BURNING BUSH) in Norwegian woods... On the bank of a sub-polar river... Mind's longing for contact with Soul... For reunion... Another 'bridge'... By the water...

'Who are you talking to?', She sings to me from Sphere of White Light surrounding Her figure. Some five metres below me. Is it still Her legs swinging in the water or is it already a piscine-tail? 'Nobody!', I sing back loudly. Surprised by clear emission of my voice. Not disturbed by any gargling or bubbling. 'Nobody.', I mutter under my breath. Very quietly...

*

We've been diving for half an hour. Deeper and deeper into blackness. I've been breathing peacefully all Time. Inhaling Water of Life. Like millions years ago...?

Diving is like flying. But we can stay much longer under water than in the air. 'The knack in learning to throw yourself at the ground and miss". Hilarious. If I had Adams's lightness in dealing with 'Life, the Universe and Everything', my opening passages would have been much more digestible.

I used to have that dream... I jump up and start 'flapping' my arms. And I just fly away. Sometimes I need to 'flap' harder to stay in the air. On another occasion a single stroke sends me sky high in a sec. I look in disbelief at my friends' unsuccessful attempts to follow me.

My instructions are so clear: 'You just "flap" your arms and fly! It's so simple! Look at me!' But no matter how hard they try, it was always a total failure. I fly above calling them to join me. But they can't. So, I end up flying all alone. Unable to share my joy with anybody. I wake up sad...

'My Time
Prime Time
And the only thing that can ever kill you
Is your mind'

(YouTube: Ma.Ste. All Clear)

*

She finally reaches the bottom of the lake and waves encouragingly to me. Her luminous figure seems so small in the vast blackness around us. I land in front of Her, as majestically as Mr Neil Alden Armstrong set his foot on the Moon. I take a step forward. Now we are very close to each other. Keeping a hypnotic eye-contact. I reach out... I take Her hand in mine. Slow motion... Our lips meet... All Universe... Infinite Space... In Its profound majesty... Holds Its breath for a split second. For us... So close to Ultimate Truths... Life is a gift... I AM speechless... All Her supernatural brightness fades away. She is my wife! My Angel...

*

So, we were standing on the bottom of Wigry lake. Over 70 metres beneath the surface. In the middle of the night. Hand in hand. Swaying gently and smiling vaguely. Watching electric eels swimming/flying above. Vanishing slowly. Maste and Margarita. What were we thinking? What were we thinking...

*

Chapter 8

Pedro

It was Monday. The other Monday. He hadn't been eating or drinking anything for nearly twenty hours. Tomorrow he will only have some fruit. But he wasn't feeling weak at all. He knew that most of energy a human body got from food was then consumed in digestive processes. He was breathing peacefully and regularly. That was where his energy was coming from. The Breath of Life…

He just finished gathering the brushwood for the bonfire and got down to light it with a match. The first sheets of paper caught the flames. His affirmations written down during the day were burning green. Magic? He remembered the refrain of one of his songs: 'Charms of Life'…

'Burn burn
You flames of green
May the light
In the branches grow
Despite all toils and fatigues
May the glitters
Caress us

Then the wind
Will inspire our plexuses
Squint

Once again
Space and Time

Maybe now
The curtains will open
For a change
And we'll stand on the sun with no spots
On such day
The shadow will flatten

Burn burn
You flames of green
May the light
In the branches grow
Despite all toils and fatigues
May the glitters
Caress us

When you share your truth
Boastfully
The spell breaks
Oh you know
What really matters
In mysteries

Burn burn
You flames of green
May the light
In the branches grow
Despite all toils and fatigues
May the glitters
Caress us'

Pedro was watching the fire with moderate interest. But every gaze of his beautiful brown eyes at his master was full of absolute admiration. The dog loved the man with all his canine heart...

He couldn't understand what his master saw in the fire. Rummaging about in bushes and speeding across meadows or between trees was so much more attractive. Bored with the fire ritual, the dog decided to go for a swim.

The night was moonless and all stars switched off for good. Leaving the whole world plunged into impenetrable darkness. The man was staring right into the fire. Feeding on its energy. He had just finished his White Light meditation. Looked around. The dog had been gone for about an hour already.

Suddenly, the man heard a distant splash ain the west part of the lake. He whistled loudly. But the black air echoed with silence. He got back to his fire watch. Twenty minutes later – another splash. A few hundred metres to the east.

'Pedro! Here!', he cried into the night. Nothing. Apparently, the dog couldn't find the way to the shore disorientated by darkness. Or maybe he spotted some mysterious reflections in the depths of the lake...

A few more cries and whistles, and the unfortunate swimmer finally emerged from the nearby reeds. Exhausted but happy. Wagging his tail sweepingly and barking joyously. The man gave him a big hug, stroking his wet head (wondering if the dog had been diving), and patting him all over his black back – b(l)ack. Then the man went on watching the fire. The dog did the same for a while, but soon got bored...

And every time Pedro was bored, but only next to a bonfire, he masturbated. Due to the obvious anatomic conditioning, he was just rubbing the erected canine penis against his own stomach, occasionally brandishing it in the air, with all the black and brown body dancing in movements clearly simulating the act of copulation...

Exhausted with the ride, the dog sat down next to his master. At last peaceful enough to focus on watching the fire. Suddenly, he raised his head and looked at the man with something very peculiar in his brown eyes... The loner could swear that Pedro's eyes were sparkling with all stars...

'You promised to tell me about Derek and Jack', She barked looking at Her master with amusement. Waiting...

*

'Did you enjoy the ride?' I couldn't help smiling.
'You know what? Your dog is a real weirdo! Just like you...'. She was gazing at me through Pedro's brown eyes, now brighten up with a warm mockery.
'Truly, pets become like their masters', She concluded.
'Or vice versa!' I remarked foolishly.
'Anyway, it was another experience for me...'
We were sitting in silence for a while.
'You know, I think he is a virgin.' I said, trying to gather my thoughts. 'He did manage to disappear for a whole night once or twice, but he is such a drip that I doubt he ever succeeded in getting laid.'

We were watching the fire. Burning out slowly. I believe it was when I saw the sparkles in the dog's brown eyes a minute ago that the stars in the sky switched back on, and were now twinkling fabulously, making the lake surface shimmer in their mysterious light. The dimmer the fire flames, the brighter the starlight – as if my bonfire was transmitting its energy to contribute to the big picture. To confirm its oneness with the whole, infinite universe.

I like the intense golden light of the embers when the last flames are about to go out. This is the 'proper gold'. The real treasure. 'My preciousssss...'

'oooooOOOOOOOOOOOOOOOOOOOOOOOOOOOO OOMMMMMmmmmm...'
The name of God in action (I AM), which I sang monotonously many times, making my brain generate theta waves, travelled from my mouth in all directions. But it was carried farthest by the lake surface in front of me. It couldn't be heard by the contemporary users and guests of the Post-Camaldolite Monastery, a gem of the local historical architecture, raised in the seventeenth century on the hill of a Wigry lake island (now a peninsular), over ten kilometres away. Though sometimes I felt as if the Camaldolese monks from the past were joining my one-syllable mantra with their chants and prayers. As if the difference between the present and the past was the same as between a meditation and a prayer. The former being a wordless equivalent of the latter.

I stood up from my semi-lotus position (will I ever learn to sit properly for my meditations?), stretched, picked up my stuff (the axe and the blanket), and started walking up slowly towards the car. The dog followed me lazily.

At the top of the hill I took the last look at the lake beneath me... Then up into the sky, to watch the breathtaking performance of the infinite universe: frantic dance of enchantingly twinkling dots of White Light. Right before my amazed eyes. Yet, I did keep breathing. The rare spectacle did not manage to take all my breath away. And I felt profoundly that I was so much (I AM) a part of all. The vivid and reassuring glitter of the stars and the glowing flame in my Heart were one and the same thing.

I was standing there for a long while. With my neck craned and my mouth open. Then I looked at Pedro... But he wasn't there... Not any more... And She was speechless...

*

Chapter 9

Wooden Car

Derek and Jack... My best friends and neighbours. The former living on the ground floor, and the latter right below me, on the third floor. Both my age and both sharing the same dubious pleasure of once being Dr Richard's patients. We were just ordinary kids, and our lives and adventures were nothing special at all. But I think I know why She insists on hearing about them. I believe She wants me to see myself in the early social context: in my initial relations with other people. She knows me too well. Better than anybody else. And She hopes that my verbalization of these memories will distract me from my egocentric tendencies.

It would be so if She were not beyond everything. She, as Sphere of White Light, a fragment of Centre of Pure, Unconditional and Everlasting Love, is beyond any intentions. Including the one to make me confess that I am such a reserved, self-contained, stuck up, pathologically extreme individualist, who does not go to concerts because for him even a trio to perform with on stage is too big a crowd. And being among audience: hundreds or thousands of foreign auras to intermingle with his – an unbearable would-be experience!

I confess that, like the lyrical subject of 'The Wall', I have developed a hard shell. And even though this whole 'writing thingy' is apparently meant to soften it, my sharing of emotions still bends under the carapace of the opening passages, which are the armour this book apparently must have been enclosed in.

*

We went to the same primary school. The first day was a nightmare. All desks were double and Derek sat with Jack. I was crying for hours demanding that either I would be sitting with one of them or I would be going home. And I went home. With my mother: a helpless witness of that embarrassing scene.

It took us a few days to find a compromise: shifts. One day I was sitting with Derek, the next with Jack. Followed by the day when the two were sitting together and I with a stranger. That was the worst shift. I always found it difficult to make new friends. And if I made one, soon I usually grew too involved. Too attached. I faced the same problem later on in my relationships with women. I mean excessive attachment. Not shifts.

I think I spent more time with Derek, especially after Jack moved with his family to another block of flats. Some 300 metres away. Yet it was Jack who infected me with his and his elder brother's fascination for hard rock music. And it was him who used to challenge my courage with unexpected attacks on me. As Kato in *The Pink Panther*. Only I had never asked for that. Once, while we were playing soccer (I was a goalkeeper as usual), all of a sudden he threw sand into my eyes and punched me on the face. I didn't fight back, pretending to be a pacifist. Little coward.

It was also Jack who 'put me to sleep' by pressing my chest with his hands for about a minute, while I was standing against the wall of the school corridor. I remember the funny feeling of being on the verge of losing consciousness. I had never experienced anything like that before. Everything blurred and I saw myself slowly sinking and falling down on the floor. It didn't last long, and soon another classmate of mine, still laughing, was getting ready for the 'experience'.

Jack was a born warrior. He became an air-force pilot in his adult life. Though had to give up after a few years due to a minor heart disease. I was a brave knight only in my childhood's imaginary world. Or when I got totally blotto, almost every night during my university 'studies'. No, I wasn't a brave knight then but a fierce, bloodthirsty barbarian from the most gloomy recesses of my mind. I was having 'fun' all night but the following morning could remember only the first few bottles of vodka. And with my tonnes-weighing head I listened to my roommates' reporting the previous night's stunts and high jinks. To my growing terror. I needed six or seven beers, sometimes ten if the distress was too overwhelming, to shake it off and get ready for another coming party. It was a miracle I survived all that madness.

*

It's a beautiful July morning. I'm sliding down the handrails in the staircase of our block of flats. Somewhere half way through I start whistling the agreed signal: Soviet National Anthem... I'm eight and a half, and have no idea that Soviet secret police executed my grandfather 27 years ago, in nearby Giby village, together with other 600 victims. I just kind of like the melody...

Derek appears in his flat entrance door just when I'm landing on the ground floor. He can always hear my whistling, as it is very quiet in our flats in 1972's Poland. TV starts in the afternoon. And the only noise-emitting device working at this time of the day (when our parents are at work and nobody is listening to the radio) is a fridge. We don't even have stationary phones. If we had I would have just given him a bell to say that I'm coming down.

We go to the basement to continue our new project. Yesterday I dismantled my brand new toy car and tore out its small engine. We needed it for the car we had designed ourselves earlier. It will be made of wood... Owing to his inborn manual dexterity, Derek has already managed to cut out one side of the car, some front and rare elements and the roof. I can feel the shape of the small engine protruding from my pocket. We are going to install it in a bit and finish the project. Hopefully today.

*

Although we've been trying for an hour the engine doesn't want to start. Soon we get bored with the project, and leave the useless, nonworking piece of junk – badly patched wooden elements – promising ourselves to work on it tomorrow. But we never do and I end up with a broken, brand new toy car in my room. Just another smash up of my incurable fantasizing with ruthless reality...

We go out to play basketball. Not having proper backboard, we aim at a hollow above the entrance of our block of flats. And then off to the playground to compete in swing-jumping.

The trick is to slip off the bench of the s̶ second before it reaches the maximum inclination. Semblance of flying. The air is s̶ Everything is...

*

I was very close with Derek. He was my true friend. We didn't talk much. We didn't have to. Understanding each other without a word. The ties of our friendship seemed quite supernatural sometimes, when, for example, Derek would walk out of his flat a moment before I started whistling.

One winter evening, we thought we spotted some extraordinary activity on the Moon's surface and decided to build a telescope to examine it carefully. Not a big deal: two different-size magnifying glasses (I must have destroyed something again probably to get them) wrapped up in a piece of cardboard, 40 centimetres apart. Oddly enough, the Moon seemed at least four times bigger when we looked at it through our new 'scientific instrument'.

The hyperactivity of the Moon's surface turned out to be false alarm, and I noticed that after watching the Earth's natural satellite for two minutes, Derek lowered the telescope and fixed the lenses on something in front of him, focusing. Our observatory was in Derek's living room, with the window facing the playground. He was looking at something right behind it. I took over the telescope (he gave up somewhat reluctantly) and pointed it in the same direction. I saw the familiar balcony... Our classmate, Jane, my beloved co-dweller of the little one windowed house, my platonic lover from the daydreaming sessions – was living in the opposite block of flats. And when I was watching her now, she was talking to her younger sister in their bedroom.

/alking about slowly. Stretching. Yawning... Finally, the girls decided to go to bed and started taking their clothes off...

The two young 'astronomers' couldn't help snatching the telescope from each other's shaking hands, until the light in the room behind the playground went out... Truly, scientists can know only as much as their instruments can measure.

*

Chapter 10

Frank

'You forgot about something'. My cat Frank, a Turkish van, snow-white long-haired fur, an absolutely perfect creature, though deaf as a post – is looking at me, with sparkles of all stars in his clear, blue sclerotic eyes.
'What?' I'm trying to recall names of talking cats I know...
'Your short-sightedness,' She mews, Frankly speaking...
'Ah yes... When they gave me the first eye test at school I was trying to convince the oculist that the cow she was pointing at was actually a duck. To my classmates' justified amusement.'
'And to Your embarrassment...'
'Humiliation! I hated those tests.'
'And then you chose to squint at the blackboard for eight years instead of wearing the glasses...'
'True. I gave up finally in the secondary comprehensive school. Do you think my short-sightedness could be one of the reasons for my disappointment with physical reality surrounding me and for my partial withdrawal from it for the sake of retrospection, introversion and self-exploration?'
'What do YOU think?'
'I never needed glasses to save my beloved from the little one-windowed house of mine. I walked over the "bridges" with my eyes closed.

Yes, I'm sure my short-sightedness did affect many of my decisions and choices.'
'Fortunately, you are not short-sighted as far as supernatural perception is concerned', She purrs with consolation.
'What do you mean?'
'I must admit you see quite a lot despite your sight defect.'
'Do I?'
'Mmmmmm...' Frank arches his white back and starts 'kneading' the inside of my elbow bend with dogged determination. This is an atavistic reflex triggered by his recollection of feeding on his mother's teats. When more pushing meant more food. H's purring loudly...

I stroke his soft white fur with affection. Cherishing the moment.
A half-blind man with a stone deaf cat on his lap...

*

Chapter 11

Bike

When I was fourteen and a half I went for a bicycle ride with Derek and Jack. We rode to Gawrych Ruda and were speeding along the winding paths alongside Wigry lake shoreline. The rush of the air on my face was blowing thoughts out of my head. Clearing my mind. When it was all empty, it started filling with the blissful White Light of Pure, Unconditional and Everlasting Love. Heaven on Earth.

A few hours later we raced at full speed into our housing estate. I was a little behind Derek and Jack and decided to ride across a huge puddle, which they were cautiously detouring. Unfortunately, on the other side of the puddle, one of the big hexagonal concrete blocks of the road pavement had caved in. And the edge of the block behind it was protruding portentously right below the surface of the murky waters.

When the front wheel of my bike hit the treacherous underwater structure, it just broke off the fork and flew up into the air behind me. This resulted in my handle bars' immediate contact with the ground.

My arms were too weak to withstand the impact and I churned my way amongst the concrete blocks with my nose. My head kissed the ground (a)gain. The element of Earth.

Derek and Jack helped me find the way home. I didn't see much from under the streams of blood flowing down my face. Washing it in the bathroom didn't help much. But I decided not to go to the doctor. On the following day my face was one big scab. Although it was tempting to go to school to scare my schoolmates and teachers, I decided to stay at home and play the guitar For a few days. Without any singing though, as I couldn't open my mouth at all. I still have a little scar on the left side of my nose: a thin, blue, vertical line. As if someone marked me out with a pen...

*

Just an accident I thought then. But now I know that there are no accidents at all. Nothing happens without a reason. Law of Cause and Effect applies All Time. Here's a list of some of the 'forces' that contributed the situation described above (my churning the concrete):

I was absent-minded. Thinking about the bliss I had experienced just half an hour before in Gawrych Ruda. About the future of my friendship with Derek and Jack. That was the end of our last year in primary school and our last trip together. Our last joint adventure ever...
'(...) Life is what happens to you while you're busy making other plans (...)', as Mr John Lennon sang in his *Beautiful Boy (Darling Boy)* two years later. A few months before his tragic death.

I was ambitious. Determined to overtake my friends. To prove to them that I was as good. No prospective danger could distract my competition spirit. It is ambition that is blind. Not love or justice.

My father is very economical. What else can you expect from a professional economist. He al(l)ways has his feet firmly fixed on the ground. He bought me that old, second-hand bicycle (which was in bad technical condition) to save money for more important expenditures. Some bills probably. Those were hard times for our family. Every month my father had to borrow money a week after he had been paid his salary. He just took another rational decision. Actually, I've al(l)ways envied him the common sense. He's really good at money management. While I'm a dreadful spender.

The road-menders neglected their duties. They should have levelled the concrete blocks. Besides, if it were a housing estate in a more civilized country, the road wouldn't be turning into a pool every time it rained. And it did even after a minor fall.

Of course, there were many more 'forces', operating from many different directions at that particular moment of time, including those from other dimensions probably, which I will never know. But no matter how detailed the description of the context of my crash, no matter how thorough the explanation of all political, social, economic and mental conditioning – the Truth is al(l)ways simple: there are no accidents. End of story.

*

Chapter 12

Sea

The sea is rough this morning. High wave. Strong wind. I like it most that way: the opposite of peacefulness of lake waters. And when the sea is rough, my lake eels surrender totally to sea snakes. Thrilled with excitement...

The sky is so blue. Rare white cloudlets being chased off rapidly. The Sun rules. When I was meditating and swimming a couple of hours ago, He was still struggling with the horizon. And now has dominated it completely.

I'm walking with Maggie, hand in hand, on the beach in Little Geese. I, my sister, and my parents discovered this place in the mid 1980s. We had been driving west along Baltic seaside, looking for something wild and remote. Little Geese welcomed us with their peace and quiet. And absolute beauty. We put up our big tent at the entrance to the beach. The narrow path cutting through the dunes took us to the sea in seconds. Many times during the day.

*

Little Geese are very special to me. Even a few days here make me a brand new man. Meditation and swimming in the morning. Meals with family. Sunbathing and more swimming during the day. Jogging and Tibetan rituals after dinner...

'Run run
Bare feet on beach sand
Face in sparkles and glitters
Sea waves prana

Step step
Pulse speeding up
Breath breath
Pain easing
Divine atomic gift

Sun sun
Concerto on eyes
Blood blood
Roaring with symphony
World dancing

Fly fly
Heart beat
Wind wind
Wings inspired
Universe dancing

Time time
Eternity
Wish wish
Rejuvenation
Immortality

Sun sun
Concerto on eyes
Blood blood
Roaring with symphony
World dancing'

(YouTube: Ma.Ste. Energia)

Hi high
Sun son
Hart heart
Beet beat

Won't want
Meet meat
Sole soul
Been bean

Peak peek
Sweet suite
Be bee
Bare bear

And then my beautiful concluding open fire on the beach every night. Regardless of the weather.

Charms of Life...

'Burn burn
You flames of green
May the light
In the branches grow
Despite all toils and fatigues
May the glitters
Caress us

Then the wind
Will inspire our plexuses
Squint

Once again
Space and Time

Maybe now
The curtains will open
For a change
And we'll stand on the sun with no spots
On such day
The shadow will flatten

Burn burn
You flames of green
May the light
In the branches grow
Despite all toils and fatigues
May the glitters
Caress us

When you share your truth
Boastfully
The spell breaks
Oh you know
What really matters
In mysteries

Burn burn
You flames of green
May the light
In the branches grow
Despite all toils and fatigues
May the glitters
Caress us'

(YouTube: Ma.Ste. Uroki Życia)

*

So, the sea is rough this morning. High wave. Strong wind. I like it most that way: the opposite of peacefulness of lake waters. And when the sea is rough, my lake eels surrender totally to sea snakes. Thrilled with excitement...

The sky is so blue. Rare white cloudlets being chased off rapidly. The Sun rules. When I was meditating and swimming a couple of hours ago, He was still struggling with the horizon. And now has dominated it completely.

I'm walking with Maggie, hand in hand, on the beach in Little Geese. Sometimes She stoops to pick up another colourful pebble. Back at home, we have many big glass jars full of such 'souvenirs' from the seaside. She shows the pebble to me. This time it's all shining black...

'You know', I speak loudly, trying to out-shout the wind, which is playing rough with Her long fair hair. 'With you the book is writing itself!'
'It is, but...' Maggie's voice. Magic voice. She smiles vaguely, squinting Her beautiful green eyes in the sunlight. The Sun is now sitting sprawled across His gold throne behind me.
'I even stopped rereading and correcting the opening passages!'
'Finally! But you know, your writing...'
'Yes?'
'It's just like your music...'
'What do you mean?'
'Do you remember "The Life Symphony In A Nutshell For The Grand Piano And The Electric Guitars"?'
'I composed it! It's all instrumental. Recorded under my Home Made Music Box project...'
'And it has twenty five parts, doesn't it?'
'Yes, it does. So what?'

'Every part is brief. There are hardly any repetitions. It sounds as if unfinished. You move from one theme to another without any warning. Even if prospective listeners managed to follow all the changes of rhythm, tempo and key, they would have no time to like any of these melodies. This piece of music, like some other of Your songs, just throws the sounds into the ear on a take-it-or-leave-it basis.

The connections are obvious to you but all others would have to listen to the track again and again to get used to its harshness. And eventually to start enjoying the individual bits of music 'stuck' together.'

(YouTube: Ma.Ste. The Life Symphony In A Nutshell For The Grand Piano And The Electric Guitars)

I think to myself that Maggie wouldn't have been able to say so much so quickly against such a strong wind. And I'm right. When She started talking the wind subsided and the wounded Sun collapsed to His knees and dipped His blood-red crown in the sea waters on the horizon. Now we are standing in this absolutely extraordinary light of His setting... The sunning set... Hypnotized by His vague, farewell shining...

'I was writing it for twenty five years. Every "bit" of this instrumental piece represents, more or less, one year of my life', I start explaining slowly. 'There are no repetitions here, as nothing happened twice in my life for twenty five years. And it never does. The river keeps flowing, and all déjà vu "feelings" are just lapses or tricks of mind...'
'And the Universe holding Its breath? Or someone being "speechless"? Or the "slow motion"?'

'I mean physical dimension. Not spiritual experience. And life is like a roller-coaster. It doesn't give us any warning before a next sudden turn.'
'So maybe You should call the book: "The Life Symphony In A Nutshell" then?'
'Maybe I will.'
'Your literature is scrambled and scrimmaged as some of your music.'

'Yes, but even if this book is as inconsistent as "The Life Symphony In A Nutshell", prospective readers don't have to "scan" it. They don't have to "swallow" it at one go. They can "digest" it slowly. Adjusting their thinking processes to the "rhythm", "tempo" and "key" accordingly...'
'Yes,' She smiles ironically, 'and you could preface the book with a letter of instructions like this:
"Dear Reader,
Please read this book slowly. Scan-reading is strictly prohibited. Stop after every passage to think. Read it again. And again, if necessary, to get the point. If there is any... If not, try to read between the lines. And please don't panic! This is just the end of the world as You know it..."'
'Would you please stop sneering,' I fake an insult, but can't help smiling.
'You know I'm not a storyteller...'
'Yes, you claim to be a vision-thrower,' She interrupts. 'Whatever that could mean. And you hope to become a storm-bringer. But I can't see any storm coming, can you?' She doesn't ask. 'I know this is supposed to be some kind of an experiment. A quasi-literary, hyper-sincere, self-psychoanalytic, progressive and intuitive writing. Fiction that reads like non-fiction Or vice versa. Literary non-fiction.

With elements of esoteric Gnosticism. Combining prose and poetry. Featuring literature with echoes of music somewhere in the background. Linking physicality with spirituality. Aiming at being both personal and universal. But you know what? I think this is all just too raw. Too chaotic. Too digressive...'
'Will you leave something for critics...'
'Who?'
'Nobody...'
'And no dialogues until I speak up finally in Chapter 7...'
'You could have started talking earlier...'
'If you had ever let me... Anyway, I think you should stick to short forms. Some of Your songs sound not bad, actually. With the structure of lyrics meeting the common standards: a few stanzas and a refrain. You are good at succinctness, throwing few words casually. But when it comes to longer passages, you get bored too quickly. Your descriptions are just hints...'
'The "stream of sub-consciousness"? Breaking all the rules? An anti-book?', I butt in shyly in self-defence.
'If you ever had any readers they wouldn't even know what Derek and Jack looked like.'
'YOU are talking about the looks? And who said "I look what you make me"? Isn't appearance irrelevant?'
'Of course it isn't. Although it can be deceptive, you must not neglect the physicality. Even if you are as spiritual as you think you are... And... And why do you endeavour so much to be original? To be different from others? You don't like pop music only because too many people listen to it!'
'As if I were hearing my wife...'

We look at each other and burst out laughing.
'Burst out laughing?', She looks into my eyes with all stars sparkling in Hers. 'And what happened to LOL?'

'I hereby officially demand you to stop eavesdropping and commenting on anything which is outside quotation marks.'
'You got it!'
'OK. Maybe you are right. Maybe I'll stick to my song-writing. But first, I must finish this... Even if this is just another meaningless undertaking. Even if nobody will ever read it, I w'll finish it! With or without you!'
'U2?'
'No, We2 or I1. And shut up, will you!'

*

Derek had fair, curly hair and blue eyes. Snub-nosed. Well-built. Medium height. Always smiling. Jack was dark-haired. With brown, smart-looking eyes. Thinner than Derek and a bit taller... That's all I remember. Forty years is a long time... Aha, and Dr Richard was definitely red-haired...

*

'Why are you laughing?' I take a long on Her face. It's being caressed by warm golden lights of our open fire flames. We are sitting on the beach. Facing the sea. I AM taken in by its salty, tempting scent and soothing, mysterious swoosh of the surf.
'Sometimes you are quite funny, actually...'
'Am I? But jokes are not allies of a serious message...'
'Bullshit!', She interrupts, smiling. But Her eyes haven't stopped laughing yet.
'I don't understand why you wanted to hear about Derek and Jack again. You know them much better than I. Just like all stories from my childhood.

Was it really to make me see myself in the early social context? It didn't work, did it? And what about the spirituality and the "bridges", which seem to be the key subject of this book? My recollections of Derek and Jack didn't throw any new light on that area either, did they?"

'Nope. I just kind of like those two blokes, I guess. That's all.'

'Yes, but what if you are right about my writing? And what if this book will end up as the... wooden car I failed to make with Derek?'

'Oh just sod off!' And She starts laughing again...

*

Chapter 13

Parents

I wonder why English grammar stopped expanding on tenses at one point, satisfied with sixteen only. Since we have Past Perfect Tense to relate what had happened before a event described in Simple Past, there should also be an Even More Distant Past Perfect Tense to be used when someone had had done something before what had happened...

*

Father and son were digging in the garden. Both grey-haired. Junior balding: losing the genetic battle inside his poor hair roots inherited from ancestors on his mother's side. Senior still in good shape, though weaker and weaker every year...

Father had been hiring that little garden from Gardens for Workforce Organization for over thirty years. He had raised a little bower there, with some help from his son, and had planted some fruit-trees.

It was another spring. Time to sow the patches with vegetable seeds again. But first the soil had to be scarified: stimulated to have high yielding in a couple of months. The two men were digging their spades into the ground unhurriedly.

*

Junior couldn't remember when he had started to like working in the garden, which had had been just another boring duty for him before. Now it felt right to get a little tired, and breathe in fresh air faster than normal, next to the next of kin.

'So, did it ever occur to you after my accident that buying me such an old bicycle had not been a good idea?', asked the son, having stopped digging, a little out of breath, to lean on the spade handle. He looked into his father's grey eyes, where he could see that little boy from a faded, black and white photo in the family album, with a pair of skates hanging over his shoulder, and Puńsk lake frozen behind him.

Puńsk is a little village where Senior had had had been brought up during World War II. Before the war, his family members had had had had been the only citizens of Polish nationality living there. 98% of the total population had had had had been Jewish. After the war, the number of Jews inhabiting the village had had had totalled... zero.

*

Junior had sometimes had that dream. He had been walking around Puńsk from an alternative, warless reality. With all the Jews still living there. Building new, bigger houses. In his dream, the village had grown into a little town. Busy and colourful. With modern urban areas...

In real life, the rule of communicating tubes al(l)ways applies. The empty village had had had soon filled up with immigrants from Lithuania. Senior's family members had had had been then the only Poles among the Lithuanian community living there.

All still feeling pretty dizzy after another turn of history...

Senior had had grown fast. Al(l)ways smart and economical. The only owner of a motorcycle and a record-player in the village. Soon he had had met his future wife. She had had been looking for a job far away from her home village: Krasnybór, as her father had had had been executed for alleged anti-soviet activity. The couple had had soon moved from Puńsk to Soovowkey, thirty kilometres away, to start a life on their own. To prepare for welcome of their first-born.

*

Time passes
Bringing His daughter
Change
Letting Law of Cause and Effect
Apply
God in action
Love

*

'Not really', father replied, gasping for air and wiping the sweat from his forehead...

Like father like son. Heste and Maste. Standing together on the surface of the globe. Nearly five thousand kilometres from its iron core. Over a hundred and fifty million kilometres from the sun. Speeding around the latter at more than a hundred thousand kilometres per hour. Looking at each other. And smiling...

*

My parents. Emotional 'umbrellas'. Always overprotective. Their caring often became interfering. But I didn't mind it. And I don't even now. When they tell me what I have done wrong, I surrender voluntarily to the parental disapproval syndrome. Happy that they are still strong enough to bother at all...

What I do mind is their eyes' becoming dull. Losing the glitter which reflects Soul's flame burning in Heart. Of(f) course, it is not Soul that chooses to fade away while we grow old. She is beyond any choices. Except the one She makes in Domain of Absolute to participate in physical dimension, where She just keeps glowing. Loving and blessing.

It is mind that turns away from Soul. Especially during our senility years. Emotionally corrupted and broken, disappointed with the physicality it has been focused on and excessively attached to, mind neglects Soul's White Light and its Wave Vibration. It forgets about the unity of the three basic elements of being. And the Oneness is necessary for rejuvenation and longevity.

Unfortunately, mind chooses to live only by itself. Indulging in recollections. Sometimes making the body as immobilized and dependent as it used to be right after the birth. To complete the circle. What can Soul do then? Being 'pushed out' by mind. Mind kills both physical body and itself. Every death is a suicide. Soul leaves. Experienced and blessing...

*

Many times did I try to explain to my parents all the basics of the rejuvenation and longevity. But they just laughed and told me to look around and see that everybody grew old, got ill and died. Everybody!

Everybody? No, they didn't want to hear about Great Masters of Being. They knew only One. And He had died. On the Cross. Yes, He did resurrect his physical body then, but He was God Son. No. it didn't matter that he had said that we were all God's Children...

I gave up finally at my grandma's funeral. Her daughter, and my mother, was kneeling at the fresh grave. Every time I recall that moment I can't help picturing her at the bottom of a ten-metre wide pit, with tonnes of black earth around. Suddenly, she cried to me heartbreakingly: 'You see?!' And I was speechless...

*

The fear of my parents' ever dying has been accompanying me in all my emotional life. It must have been one of my first conscious thoughts. Generated soon after my mind had recorded the two trembling shadows on the wall bending over my bed with affection. Even now, at least once a month, I dream that one of them dies. And when I wake up, the relief soon turns into a worry: some day it will be it. And I won't be able to wake up...

For many years after my other grandpa died of lung cancer, every x-ray test of my chest was a nightmare. Cancer: one of modern world's major killers. It has replaced wars in preventing the world's overpopulation. Together with car accidents, AIDS, and many other outcomes of mind's projection. What can we do? We only have two choices: either to 'wait for the hammer to fall' or to explore the subject thoroughly and find solutions.

Don't worry about this thoroughness. Some other time. Now just a few hints. First of all, it is about genetics, of(f) course. Karma. We inherit genes responsible for our inclinations to the given illnesses. Then it's our choices. If your grandpa dies of a lung cancer and you become a chain smoker at the age of ten – you choose to die too early. If you eat dead animals, to let their foreign protein intermingle with yours inside your precious body – you choose to die too early.

If you drink beer and vodka, smoking weed all through, every day for years, and keep telling everybody that you want to live fast and short, boasting of your nothing-to-lose desperado life style – you choose to die too early. If you are like a herring in a shoal, following others in everything – you choose to die too early, as everybody around you gets ill, grows old and dies. If you can't see (hear, to be exact) the original unity of Soul, mind and the body – you choose to die too early. If you can't understand Law of Cause and Effect and you keep living unconsciously – you choose to die too early.

And when is it too early? Al(l)ways.

*

Of(f) course, physical immortality is not a target but an alternative. And to live consciously means to be aware of as many options as possible and to make choices based on such awareness. However, you should realize that responsible living is only the beginning of the process of shaping our reality.

A thought travels from the 'tip of the iceberg' conscious mind = surface mind = 'combined laboratory & library in the head' = 'i am', w every morning and vibrating/echoing all over the brain throughout the day') down under to reach the deep layers of the real decision-making mechanism: subconscious mind.

Techniques for sending signals from the 'surface' to the 'depths' include conscious breathing, fasting, meditation and visualization. However, our choice is only one of many 'forces' which operate at the given moment, contributing to overall outcome of the given event, affecting a situation. But decisions of our deep mind regarding surface mind and physical body surpass all other 'forces'. And those regarding our Soul are final...

*

I wish my parents would choose to join me in my spiritual exploration. I wish they would decide to take up the rejuvenation and longevity. The latter doesn't make sense without the former, of(f) course. I wish my mother would learn to swim and ride a bike finally. Even at the age of eighty or something. I wish I didn't think that I should have rather used Simple Past tense after all the above 'I wish's'. Wishful thinking...

Wishing is all I can do really. I can't even persuade my sons that eating meat is bad for them. Will they blame me in the future for my not being strict enough with them about it now. If they ever go on vegetarian diet. Maybe I should just make them give up this barbarian habit. But wouldn't it be a violation of their freedom of choice? We all have free will. Though freedom ends where our decision would lead to hurting other people.

Therefore, I choose to avoid enforcement of any 'spiritual imperatives'. Instead of telling my wife, children, parents and other people what they have to do to live a better life, I just keep setting a good example. That's what I believe it is anyway.

Whatever my parents decide to do, I'll al(l)ways love them, remembering how I rushed to sit on my father's lap. Cuddling up to him and hugging my mother, sitting beside. My emotional 'umbrellas'. I am so happy and grateful to God, who is Law of Cause and Effect, for letting me enjoy their company for so long. When I look around I think it's a real miracle. I've been so lucky...

*

'And he said unto another, "Follow me." But he said, "Lord, suffer me first to go and bury my father." Jesus said onto him, "Let the dead bury their dead: but go thou and preach the kingdom of God".
(Luke 9:59-60)

*

Chapter 14

Japan

'Wishful thinking?' She wonders, glancing incredulously from behind Mr Shoko Matsumura's glasses, with his slanting, navy blue young eyes. We are on Shinkansen, a Bullet Train, travelling from Tokyo to Nagoya...
'I remember that song', She continues. 'But the lyrics don't have anything to do with the hopes for Your parents' "conversion". You just keep singing...'
'Please don't...', I try to stop Her, but it's too late. She begins singing to herself, imitating Mr Matsumura's Japanese accent. Mount Fuji joined us on the south soon after we left Tokyo and still keeps company. Even though we are speeding at 300km/h for quite some time already.

'I'm gonna fuck my lady
Fuck my lady tonight
And it's gonna be cool
And it's gonna be so cool

I'm gonna screw my baby
Screw my baby alright
And she's gonna be fine
And she's gonna be just fine'

(YouTube: Ma.Ste. Wishful Thinking)

'My wife never liked this song. So, I changed all the "fucks" into "hugs"' and replaced all the "screws" with "kisses"', I remind Her.
'No wonder. And I should reconsider everything I said before about "complexity" of your artistic output.' She states, beaming.

'You know, sometimes one just has to let all the "smartness" and "sophistication" relax a little...' I excuse myself uncertainly.
'Sure. Too much elaboration leads to collaboration.'
'What do you mean?'
'I don't know I've just made it up.'
'Does it have any deeper implications?'
'Maybe, but I don't have a clue what they might be. The "stream of sub-consciousness"?'

The sunlit volcanic massive of Mount Fuji keeps stuffing clumsily through the window. As if trying and failing to grasp any sense in this conversation.

'Maybe...'
'Anyway... I wanted to ask you about something from the preceding passage. About Soul leaving physical body. You believe that subconscious mind finally "pushes" Soul out of physical body, right? And out of brain, where mind "dwells". So, every death is a suicide. Well... That's not what God tells Neale Donald Walsch. About Soul's sole decision to leave physical body. And mind.'
'First of all, if my book is ever going to be published, both Mr Walsch and Mr Leonard Orr will definitely sue me for stealing their ideas...'
'Wait a minute. Now seriously for a moment. Firstly, these two gentlemen are enlightened human beings, who happily welcome any followers. Secondly, you are not "stealing" anything from them. They write about universal things, Ultimate Truths, which do not belong to them.

They didn't invent conscious breathing, fasting, Oneness of Soul, mind and body or physical immortality. They just discovered them. Both for themselves and for others.
Finally, aren't you telling your own, original story? And in your own way? Even if some of our dialogues may resemble Walsch's conversations with God, the rest of the book is totally different from his writing. And do you remember Orr's motto? Love truth and simplicity. Simplicity!'
'What do you mean? Some of my songs are very simple. Take "Wishful Thinking"'...
'You know what I mean.'
'Maybe. But I can't agree with you that my "beliefs" stand in contradiction to the contents of Mr Walsch's Conversations with God.'
'O rly?'
'I think what he calls Soul's "decision" is the final result of subconscious mind's choices. Soul is White Light Wave which pervades all our physical body, concentrating in Heart Chakra, where the Flame glows most intensively. Soul always says: "Yess". At the moment of death, subconscious mind says: "Go". And the Soul says "Yess". Maybe adding a farewell 'You know I love you'. We might as well call it Soul's "decision". But I wanted to avoid the word "decision" as I had written before that Soul was BEYOND any conditioning, any choices, any decision-making processes valid for physical relativity. I mentioned that the only "decision" She made was in Domain of Absolute. Where She chose to detach from Grand Sphere of White Light, which represents Centre of Pure, Unconditional and Everlasting Love, in order to participate in physical dimension. Do you remember my naïve vision from the Beginning?'
'Sure. Aren't you hungry?'

*

It is 1993. I am Office Director of Soovowkey Chamber of Commerce and a participant of the Study Course in Business Management for Poland at Japan Productivity Centre, held by the Japan International Cooperation Agency under the International Cooperation Programme of the Japanese Government.

For six weeks (from 16 November through 10 December) we learn about superiority of Japanese entrepreneurship and economy. The whole country is Kaisha (Corporation) and every citizen – its employee. With nearly 130 million smart and ambitious people living on 377,873km2 of their islands, with population density rate in Tokyo Metropolis reaching 6.000 per square kilometre (in a Shinjuku swimming pool I had about 20 Japanese 'competitors' crawling up and down my lane) – there's not much room left for individuality.

Less chance for ego's domination should make them more spiritual. If only did they have enough time for such searching and researching in what's left from their private lives. Fortunately, they don't work 7/11 anymore, but still this is probably the largest population of workaholics in the world.

*

We visit Toyota, Toyoda, Caterpillar Mitsubishi, Keiroku Industrial Co-operation, Roboto, STS, etc. They are all powerful and successful enterprises. And Tokyo's skyscrapers in Shinjuku or its young life energy of Shibuya are very impressive.

However, I prefer Buddhist temples of Kyoto, including the Golden Pavilion, Ginkaku-ji and Kiyomizu-dera; its Shinto shrines, such as Heian Jingū; its palaces, like Kyoto Imperial and Sento, day in Nagoya; and its beautiful gardens, especially Ryōan-ji – the Dry Landscape – an abstract garden, with the lonely piece of rock at one side of a neatly raked square of fine-grained gravel: a manifestation of the Zen Buddhism philosophy.

I meditate there for an hour. Contemplating mind: the rocky island, immersed in the gravel 'waters': Soul. I pray without words for reunion with the pure element or the essence of the form.

*

My first evening in Tokyo is a civilization shock. I get a credit card! We don't have any cash-machines in Poland yet, not even in Warsaw. The one a hundred metres from my hotel is now winking at me knowingly and promisingly with its flickering neon-light red-heart logo. On the way to the cash-machine I cross a street with a double road-viaduct. There are two dual-carriage ways going in the same direction above my head. One on top of the other. I have to stop for awhile to admire that three-level steel structure. A true masterpiece of road engineering.

A few months later I will start having another repetitive dream of alternative reality. Apart from the one about warless Puńsk village. This time it will be futuristic Soovowkey with glass & aluminium skyscrapers and three-level viaducts. I'll be driving around, wondering: 'Where is this street? How far is it from the centre? Or maybe this is a new city centre... But it wasn't here yesterday!'

As a youngster, I used to hope for my small, obscure town to 'catch the urban ball on the fly'. Although I did appreciate its rare, pseudo-classicistic two-storey buildings, all those busy streets from the American movies seemed so much more attractive. I still remember my enthusiasm and pride when they installed first traffic lights in Soovowkey! Or raised first 12 storey buildings.

*

However, when I am now looking up 48 storeys of Tokyo Metropolitan Government Building, craning my neck to count the 55 floors of Shinjuku Mitsui Building, or eye-climbing the walls of Sunshine 60, or admiring 333-metre high Tokyo Tower – I start missing my small town. Its peace and quiet.

As opposed to Tokyo Metropolis's roaring with all possible noises. In Soovoykey, within the reach of 10 kilometres, whichever direction, there is a lake to swim in and a forest to enjoy. Here, within the area of over 620 square kilometres, it's just streets and structures. The urban jungle...

A few years later, my Brazilian business associate will invite me to come and visit his home city: São Paulo. He will scream on the phone: 'You'll love it! The city is SO alive! When you open the window you can hear "aghrghaghrghaghrghaghrghaghrgh!!!!!" 24/7 !!!'

'No, thanks", I will think, listening to birds' trills outside my window in world's forgotten, poorly industrialized Soovowkey.

During my long walks around Tokyo, I catch myself heading for less entertaining and fashionable districts to have a glimpse of lives of ordinary Japanese people. I soon find that they are excellent drivers. It is not only manoeuvring along all those narrow and winding streets (only major roads have turned out to be wide, and just a few – three-levelled), but they can also park a car right between two posts in front of their house, even when the distance between the posts exceeds the actual length of the car by an inch!

*

One of my many observations is that their houses, for obvious reasons, are built very close to each other, sometimes only half a yard apart. And what's right in the middle? Between their outer walls? A garden! Always with a well-kept tiny lawn. Sometimes with some flowers or even vegetables. Japanese adaptation skills are just amazing...

It would have been a wonderful stay, if not my longing for the family. Especially my beautiful wife, my three-year-old first-born son and the new find: a three-month-old Alsatian...

'I know what you're thinking', I say to Mr Matsumura, watching all stars twinkling in his slanting, navy blue young but tired eyes, reflected on the inside of his glasses' lenses. We are about to arrive in Nagoya...
'What?'
'We'd better keep our physical immortality philosophy in secret here."
'Why?'

'If this clever nation starts working on it: adapting, improving and innovating, in five hundred years their population will be twenty times bigger than now! Where will they be living then?'

'You worry too much. First of all, spirituality is an individual and not a national issue, although collective Karma does contribute to the overall picture. Look at India, which despite having the biggest number of Great Masters of Being in history has one of the highest mortality rate in the world. Some individuals will "grow up" to awareness of their Divine Potential and others won't. It depends on so many factors, including Karma (or genetics if you like, same difference), political, social and economic conditioning, family and education background, and so on and so forth. It's impossible to explain why the idea of spiritual searching and researching attracts some minds while it does not appeal to others. And of course, there are many Great Masters of Being of Japanese "nationality". The quotation marks I just showed You indicate that they are citizens of the Universe and the question of "nationality" is irrelevant. It is individuality that matters, as I said before. Secondly, as you have noticed, the ambitious, technology-oriented Japanese, just as many other civilized nations, focus on their jobs. And when they come back home they just take advantage of modern technologies. They switch on all the up-to-date devices and equipment. Who needs to bother with meditation or visualisation when virtual reality offers everything at a "snap of your fingers"! You just press the button, and Your pituitary gland and hypothalamus start secreting endorphins and generating Theta waves automatically. Truly, hi-tech nations have worked out powerful "bridges". But none of them is the true BRIDGE. Except for a bathtub.

I mean although modern plumbing is not so "hi-tech", it's definitely a luxury in less civilized and underdeveloped countries. And it makes a perfect tool for conscious breathing, cleansing and meditation. Ask Mr Leonard Orr, who discovered Re-birthing while soaking in his bathtub water. Archimedes of the New Age! It is him who claims that if you have a fire place and a bathtub, and know how to use them properly, you can live forever! Finally, before physical immorality concept becomes popular, some alternative places will be available for settlement, including ocean bottom and other planets. Besides, individuals living in the same body for a thousand years must know how to see through the molecular structures of physicality and thus must know different techniques of dematerialization /re-materialization and transfiguration.
So, finding a place to stay in physical dimension shouldn't be a big deal for them. The more so that they don't need spaceships for interstellar journeys. They use inter-dimensional passages. Like your "opening passages". Don't they?'
'Are you asking me?'
'No.'
'Good.'

We are already there. Nagoya railway station. Mr Matsumura, our coordinator and interpreter, takes us to the headquarters of a big corporation. Then we have dinner with their management. Even after a few rounds of sake, the Japanese directors remain very reserved. They tell us a lot about the corporation and The Corporation but all our questions requiring any declaration of their own opinions on different aspects of life are answered somewhat reticently. And although Mr Matsumura is doing a great job as our interpreter, we still have a feeling that something is lost in translation...

*

Chapter 15

Suzie

I and Maggie were sitting in the 'green room'. I used to be our bedroom but ended up as my office. Roman blinds in the windows were pulled down, sifting the autumn sunlight, whose rays, as strings of a golden harp, were cutting the room through. In all directions...

Another brain metaphor? Mind as a whole? Both the tip and the rest of the iceberg? The Universe? With solid streaks of light as root, subconscious thoughts, which have the biggest influence on our life, our decisions and choices? And flashes of electricity: lake eels (conscious thoughts) and sea snakes (the 'bridges')?

Nah. I didn't think about it that way then. I was just holding out my right hand lazily in the air and plucking the golden strings with my enchanted fingers. The strings resounded with angelic music only Soul could hear.

'Are my opening passages really inter-dimensional?', I asked ironically.

'No, I was just playing with words. But I do like how you refer to the structural elements of the book as "passages". Not just "paragraphs". Owing to this little "trick" the expression "opening passages" could imply opening something.'
'Opening what?'
'I don't know, opening some areas of the Universe. Cutting them through. Leading somewhere.'
'Some... where to?'
'I don't know, to... a gate...'
'Like the Ninth Gate from Mr Arturo Pérez-Revete's *El Club Dumas*...?
'Or the opposite direction...'
'It'd better be the opposite direction! Otherwise New Agers will "crucify" me! We can't tell them now that all the hitherto spiritual... "stuff" has been meant to contribute to another manifestation of ideas originating from the same area where Sir Ahmed Salman Rushdie's *The Satanic Verses* come from. Who will arise me to the nobility for protection? New Agers can get pretty wild when they are angry...'
'O rly?' LOL.
'Ye rly.' LOL.
'I've just imagined all those vegetarians becoming bloodthirsty all of a sudden...'
'Please stop, jokes are not allies...'
'Oh shut up! Don't come up with that nonsense again.'

*

Maggie rested Her back on the backrest of our light pink and white narrow-stripped coach, and breathed in the golden air, vibrating with the angelic tunes. She crossed Her fabulous legs, clothed (unnecessarily) in a pair of jeans.

Have you noticed that 'jeans' and 'genes' have identical pronunciation? Although totally different spelling. Not to mention the semantics. And God knows why spelling of 'fish' has been simplified to this obvious combination of four letters: 'f-i-s-h'. The same word could have been spelt as well 'ghuiss'. With 'gh' for 'f' (as in 'enou<u>gh</u>'), 'ui' for 'i' (as in 'bisc<u>ui</u>t'), and 'ss' for 'sh' (as in pre<u>ss</u>ure).

'But seriously', She resumed, 'despite the "devilish" look in Mr Rushdie's eyes (and he doesn't "rush" to "die" at all, by the way), when you were reading *The Satanic Verses*, you didn't find anything too "diabolic" in or between them, did you?'

I was just opening my mouth to answer the question, when our other cat, Suzie, a female Persian, rushed into the room. In her mouth, she was holding a piece of aluminium foil. Set into a ball.

She is a total opposite of Frank. His fur is all white. While hers, with a little longer hair, shines with three colours: black, russet and white. His eyes are blue. Hers are brown. He is a confirmed individualist. Keeping the distance. Reluctant to surrender to caresses. Unless he initiates them. Rough player. Wild and aggressive at games. Very majestic most of the time. While she is a 'cat-nympho'. Demanding to be fondled. Laying on the carpet or on the coach, baring her tricolour furry tummy and mewing provocatively. When caressed, she 'kneads' the air with her front little paws, 'climbing in circles'... So 'corrupted'... She starts purring at you glance from a distance. As if to a recollection or expectation of pleasure.

Suzie was lying down on guard and looking at me. She was chewing the aluminium foil ball and growling like a dog. Not many cats do that When I heard that for the first time, I thought I was hallucinating. I don't believe in reincarnation as such but I couldn't help associating her growl with my memories of Pedro.

'Not to worry', Maggie tried to calm me down, having noticed astonishment mixed with anxiety in my eyes. 'Suzie's not going to say anything. Two lyrical subjects and one talking cat should be enough for such personal writing. She's here just for the retrieve.'

That was true, the dog-like cat-nympho let go of the aluminium foil ball, which landed between my feet. Firmly fixed on the carpet. I picked it up and threw into it behind the open door. Suzie sped out of the room losing her little tricolour thick-furred paws, which had hard time keeping up with her mind: impatient, already in the hall, contemplating the rolling ball, disappointed with the slowness of the body. And she had the three colours everywhere, even all over her pads.

'Although it would be interesting to have the third lyrical subject', I thought aloud, keeping the ball rolling. 'We would call ourselves: "Me", "Myself" and "I".
"It's a nice day today", says I.
"Quite lovely, indeed", agrees Myself.
'Pretty cool", adds Me.'
'Which of the names would be for me?', She wanted to know.
'Well, I would be "I", you would be "Myself", you know: "My Self", and the third lyrical subject would be "Me", I guess', I explained, beaming.

'Don't forget that we also had "i" in the opening passages. What happened to it, by the way?' She wondered.

'No idea. It just disappeared when you turned up. I mean, when I "let you speak", as you put it.'

'That IS so. I speak when you let me and I look what you make me. You're the boss! By the way... boss, I don't quite understand the concept of my "migration" from one place to another. Between past and present. Without any chronological order. And I'm not sure if it's a good idea to use past tenses for the present context and vice versa. Why do you keep putting me inside different bodies to talk to me? I find it pretty awkward sometimes, really.'

'You mean the Pedro "dance" experience.'

'Not only.'

'OK, but wasn't it you who inspired me to try to see myself in different situations? In order to let me understand myself better? Besides, there must be some truth in the saying that we are what other people think we are.'

'No, you are not interested in that, are you?', She didn't ask. 'You don't care about other people's opinion at all! Which is a good thing actually. You live to the full when you experience things yourself and make choices based on your own experience and intuition. Of(f) course, there is no point in checking out something that is not important to you. For instance, if you look better in green or in blue. For this, you can rely on somebody else's opinion. Or things which are obvious. Like what would happen if you cut off one of your fingers. But there are so many other aspects of life, which are crucial for you and absolutely worth experiencing. Especially those regarding your health and happiness. Therefore, you should not take for granted what others say about positive thinking, conscious breathing, meditation, vegetarianism, fasting, fire walking, and so on. Just go ahead and try them, for sake's sake!

Your own experience of the given thingies can be different from what you've heard. Everybody is an individual being, you know. Although there are some spiritual and emotional "imperatives", which apply always and to all.'

*

'Anyway, it must have been quite an experience for yourself... Your Self... Or rather your "i", as in "individuality" from the opening passages... To face the nation which was conditioned to such overwhelming collectiveness,' Maggie resumed, watching the fetching cat.

Suzie was running to and fro, chasing the aluminium foil ball I threw, and bringing it back. She was now glowering at me with her brown, playful eyes, waiting for another throw.

'Yes, it was.' I admitted, taking a swing and letting the retrieve object off. I sent it through the open door. From the 'green room' into the hall. 'And, honestly, I don't envy the ambitious, overworked Japanese and their civilization advancement at all. I definitely prefer more privacy and freedom to high technology and industrialization. Although I do understand the country's social, political and economic factors and respect its citizens' choices.'
'You know, your description of the trip to Japan, seems to indicate that it was a total waste. Of both Japanese and probably Polish taxpayers' money, as far as I understand the structure of the organization which arranges such study courses. You were more focused on social and spiritual aspects of Japan rather than on their business management strategies.'

'Not exactly. As you remember, I was also a diligent and active participant of the training course. Attending all classes, and listening very carefully to everything they had to say. When other participants found out that I had M.A. degree in English Philology, I was unanimously elected the 'spokesman' of the group. Responsible for thanking either lecturers or representatives of all those corporations we visited. At the end of every session or meeting. So I soon developed a little speech...'

*

'On behalf of my colleagues and myself, I would like to express our utmost gratitude for the extremely interesting lecture / heart-melting hospitality . We do appreciate Your sharing with us all your excessive knowledge and experience And we shall have plenty to praise You for when we return to our home country. Thank you very very much indeed! Domo arigato gozaimasta!'

Of(f) course, I had made up the last expression. I wouldn't have been myself if I hadn't. 'Domo arigato gozaimasta' is a cluster of two polite Japanese expressions. Used alternatively. Just like nobody would probably say "very very much indeed". But you know me. Always forcing to be original. Playing with word formation in any tongue. I'm still not quite sure if our lecturers and hosts were laughing with me or at me every time I finished my little speech of thanks.

Anyway, when I came back to Poland I met many members of Soovowkey Chamber of Commerce, to present the East Asian models of economic operations.

Well, it was not my fault that Japanese business management strategies did not match Polish economic (and social) reality at all. Especially in early 1990s.

'They didn't. No doubt. But why don't you remind me how you found the treasure...?'

*

Chapter 16

Treasure

In late sixties and early seventies, I and my sister spent most of summer holidays in our grandparents' house in Puńsk. My father's younger sister and her husband were living only a mile away. They had two children. Emily was my age and Bob – now Betty's husband – two years younger. They came over every day to play with me and Ursula in the yard behind our grandparents' house. We must have been quite inventive to have fun for hours without any toys. Or alcohol.

In summer 1972, half a year after my grandpa's death, when I was eight and a half (soon after the wooden car fiasco), I came to Puńsk with my head full of ideas inspired by that new book I had finished reading at the end of the school year: Timur and His Team by a Soviet writer, Mr Arkadi Gaydar.
The title character, Timur, a very clever boy, constructs a system of strings and bells for communication with his friends. The book was written before World War II, when telephones were not yet in common use, especially in the Soviet Union. Owing to the 'ingenious' system, when Timur wants to meet a friend of his, he just pulls the right string...

A couple of days after my arrival, the whole yard looked like a spider's web. I, Ursula, Emily and Bob, worked out a complicated system of codes for signalling different messages. One ring would mean 'Come to me'. Two rings – 'I'm coming to you'. And... that was about it basically, I suppose.

So we were sitting all day, each in a different corner of the yard, hiding in the bushes, pulling the strings, and visiting each other.

My grandma didn't mind the bells' ringing. She had heard it a lot before selling their cows. And the bells remained to become a part of my new communication system. What she did mind was the web in her yard. And every time she forgot to look down, we had another maintenance break in our game.

*

One afternoon Emily gave me a ring. Just one ring. So, I went down to her bush. To see. What she wanted. She was a pretty girl. Long dark hair. Blue eyes, sparkling with smartness and curiosity.

'What's up?' I asked, struggling through the thicket. 'It'd better be something important.' I was the boss. Of(f) course. Or Chief, if we played Indians. I sat down, with a moderately indifferent look on my face, to listen to what she had to say.
'This morning, I went to the larder behind the kitchen and found some wooden stairs going up,' she whispered conspiratorially. 'I climbed them slowly until they finished with a hatch leading to the attic.'
'I know about that hatch,' I said with confidence. Although I had even no idea there were any stairs in the larder. 'And it's not a "hatch". You watch too much The Four Tankmen And A Dog on TV'.

It was a very popular series about a crew of Polish armoured division, formed in the Soviet Union in 1943, on their combat trail to Berlin, with that Alsatian on board. 'It's the trapdoor to the loft. But it's padlocked.' I risked.
'No, it isn't. I pushed it up with my back and it let go.'
'Did you get inside?' I couldn't pretend anymore that I wasn't interested.
'No, it's all dark in there. I was scared.' she confessed.
I was considering her report for a while. She was waiting for my decision, looking at me with due respect.
'OK, we are going in there now.' I commanded and stood up.
'But we don't have a torch.' She whispered, struggling to her feet.
'I've seen one in grandma's kitchen drawer. Follow me.'
And off we went, leaving Ursula and Bob at their posts in the bushes. At the opposite corners of the yard. Ringing up and visiting each other...

*

The first object that caught my sight when I opened the drawer was a little wooden case with my grandpa's shaving items inside. I lifted its cheap-folk-curved lid, and the bottom of the oval mirror, which was hinged to the upper end of the back of the lid, swung down to rest on the edge of the case. I froze seeing myself in the mirror, remembering how it used to reflect grandpa's lathered face. Al(l)ways with the inevitable glass holder in his mouth. Loaded with a smoking, unfiltered cigarette.

He had passed away the previous year. I and Emily, his favourite grandchildren, were now looking at the cut-throat razor, a half-used tube of shaving cream and the leather sharpening belt. All neatly arranged inside the case. We were trying to grasp flashes of memories cutting our minds through. In all possible (and impossible) directions. Speechless...
Finally, I closed the case. And the case was closed. I picked up the torch from the bottom of the drawer and we went to the door behind the kitchen.

We opened it and entered the little larder. The wooden shelves inside were groaning with jars, bottles and other vessels full of grandmas' home-made delicacies. One of the walls was all covered with a heavy purple curtain. I had always thought it was hiding another frame of shelves. But my clever cousin had proven again she couldn't be deceived so easily. I stepped forward and pulled the curtain. Indeed, the stairs were right behind.

'Alright', I said. 'Let's go up.'

I climbed the old wooden stairs. Emily followed. At the top, I pushed the trapdoor. The heavy hinged lid made of solid wood let go. With my hands up, I lifted the trapdoor leaf to the vertical position and put it slowly down on the attic floor on the other side of the hinge.

I looked around. It was not all that dark inside. Late afternoon and sunning set... The setting sun shone right through the only bull's eye, in the farthest wall...

*

I stood on the dusty floor and took a step aside to let Emily climb in. Switched the torch on, since I was already holding it, and started walking towards the red-glowing eye of the bull. Emily following me.

Between the knee braces, which were sloping so sharply that ten metres of the width of the attic floor at the bottom reduced to only three metres of the length of the ridge beams, attached to the principal rafters and supported by the angle braces, at the top.

As a typical attic, the place was full of junk. Old furniture, mostly broken. Wicker baskets, loaded with items of mysterious origin and purpose. Many glass vessels, including large empty demijohns. Rolled, ancient-looking carpets and rugs. It didn't occur to us then that some of the objects might have belonged to that Jewish family our grandparents had bought the house from before World War II.

The bull's only eye was scanning everything with already dying out red, laser-like rays. Piercing the omnipresent dust, the particles of which were dancing in the air, making it alive. Despite the musty smell of all the dead staff 'interred' in this 'tomb'.

We were exploring the attic carefully. Picking up and examining some of the items which looked more interesting than others. I was shining the torch to search every darker nook and cranny for some hidden secrets. And I had that feeling again... The excitement to anticipation of finding something longed and valuable. Like the key to my father's drinks cabinet. Or presents under Christmas tree. Once again, I was joyfully expecting to unravel a mystery...

*

And there it was. In the west/south corner of the attic. Next to the fading away eye of the bull. Under a huge spider's web. I couldn't see the spider. It was the web that looked enormous. Strung between the end angle brace and the principal rafter.

'What's this?' Emily whispered, staring at our find and gripping my arm.
'A huge spider's web.' I tried to relieve the tension.
'No, I mean this thing on the floor... Oh my God! What a huge spider's web!'
'What? Can you see the spider?' I squinted my short-sighted eyes following the trembling torchlight. Scanning the whole corner area nervously.
'No. But the web is bloody huge!'
'Watch your language, little lady.' I pretended to care.
'Don't call me "little". Actually, I'm two months older than you. Better tell me what you think this might be.'

I stepped forward cautiously, looking up for any sign of the 'host' – or the 'ghost' – the '(g)host' – of the grid structure. I swept a pile of dusted curtains, or some pieces of material, from the surface of something that looked like a...

'Pirates' trunk!', Emily exclaimed, shivering with excitement. She was right.
It was a fairy-sized, ancient-looking chest.
'A trunk is a log before debarking.' I explained. 'Or a car boot, if you're American. Now this thing is a chest.'
'But it doesn't have any drawers...'
'Right... Hmmm... OK, it's a trunk alright then', I admitted.

I couldn't recall any pirates in our family. But there might have been some. Considering my love for the sea, adventure and... alcohol.

I raised the hinged lid made of solid wood, with a déjà vu feeling that I had been doing a similar thing half an hour ago. And a little earlier. Holding it ajar with one hand, I shone the torch into the depths of the trunk.

*

We were quite disappointed to see the ordinary stuff. Just some clothes, documents and books. I leaned the lid against the wall, and helped Emily search through the contents of the trunk.

All we found were some items which definitely belonged to our grandparents. Like their ancient-looking, framed yellowish photo-portraits. My mind began to seriously question the alleged origin of the trunk, when suddenly...

'A pirate-castaway's bottle!' Emily burst with enthusiasm again. She was holding a brown glass vessel in her shaking hand.
'Give it to me!' Her excitement must have been contagious.

She considered it a while. Examined the screw cap. And finally held out her hand in my direction. I took the bottle. Weighed it and tried to illuminate its contents with the torchlight.

'Hold it.' I said to her, passing the torch. 'Shine it here.'

I unscrewed the cap slowly and looked inside the bottle. I saw something...

'A letter from the pirate-castaway!' I screamed triumphantly.
'I told you!' Emily started jumping around me, beaming with happiness and joy. 'Take it out and read it, quickly!'
'A message in the bottle?' I started speaking slowly to myself, with growing doubt. 'From a pirate-castaway? In Puńsk? Three hundred miles from the sea?' Finally, I was calm again. 'It's impossible.' I concluded.
'Just read it!" Emily was getting more and more impatient. A typical hothead. While I was a phlegmatic type. Walking over the 'bridges'. Drifting in the mist. Looking inside.
I inserted my forefinger into the neck of the bottle and took out two pieces of paper...

*

No, it wasn't a letter from a pirate-castaway. And I was holding up two banknotes. 100 US dollars each. A substantial amount of money in 1972's Poland, actually. You could buy a decent motorcycle at the equivalent of 50 bucks in Old Polish Zlotys. So, we did find a treasure!

At first, we are were disappointed that our pirate-castaway's life, probably extremely adventurous, would remain secret. But then... We were rich! Having shared the spoils fifty-fifty (100/100, to be exact), we threw the bottle inside the trunk, closed it and went downstairs for supper.

We didn't tell anybody. Not even shared the course of our escapade with Ursula and Bob. They couldn't understand why the two of us smiled at each other secretly now and then and winked knowingly over dinner.

*

Back in Soovowkey, I discovered that my banknote was a bit too shabby and decided to press it. I prepared the iron and was about to start the operation, but then my friends called me from the playground to join them for a game of soccer. I left everything, promising myself to be back soon to finish the job, and went playing...

When my father got home from work and saw the steaming 'monster' next to a 100 US dollar banknote on the kitchen table, it took him a while to fix his feet back on the ground, reconnect his neurons and disconnect the iron.

Of(f) course, it turned out that my grandma had been keeping the 200 US dollars in the trunk for a rainy day. Times were hard and she was a wise woman. While I just happened to be a silly little storm bringer...

*

Chapter 17

Karen & Amanda

I have another cousin my age. Her name is Karen. As kids, we used to spend a lot of time together in her home village, which was surrounded by the most yellow sand dunes in the world. Overgrown with pine woods. I often tried to imagine how that amazing yellow must have matched red of all the blood it had been painted with. So many fighters had laid their lives there. For so many different causes brought in by tumultuous history of that area...

Karen's long blond hair was blowing in the breeze against the back of her light frock when I was chasing her around my aunt's house. I can still hear her pearl of laughter. Merry and full of innocent excitement... Her green eyes were sparkling with freshness...

My beautiful cousin seemed not to notice that I couldn't tear my eyes away from her. When she was cleaning, watching telly, listening to the radio, dancing... Every time she went out to the wooden privy at the back of the garden, I was devouring her handsome figure, with my nose pressed to the window pane. Staring at her beautifully rounded hips. Obsessed by their wonderful moves. Shameless...

Actually, I was sweet on most of my she-cousins. Especially on my mother's side. But Karen was special. My true, secret love for years. I regretted then that my little one-windowed house had been ruined by hard rock and alcohol. Karen and I would have been so happy there...

*

Amanda is at least three years younger than me. In late seventies and early eighties, we met almost every weekend we were teenagers. She used to came to Soovowkey with her mother (and my aunt). I liked sitting next to her on a bench in the playground. Smoking. Not saying much. Seeing a kind of a warm encouragement in her smiling eyes.

Owing to very good relations with her father, she was confident, understanding, respectful and open in relation to the opposite sex. If not that intriguing look in her eyes, spending Time with her would have been like fooling around with my male pals. She was my female buddy. Until one summer...

*

It was August 1982.

Eight months after General Jaruzelski's declaration of Marshall Law.

Six months after my first meeting, and falling in love with Emily's classmate: Rebecca, then my dance-partner at the ball, a passionate kisser, trying desperately to forget in my arms about her fiancé's serving in the army for too long.

Five months after the traditional school ball (held one hundred days before the final exams) which ended officially at 9.30 p.m., so that we could manage to get to our private parties (informal continuations of the event) before the curfew.

Four months after my form's playing truant (under my leadership) on the First Day of Spring (which was strictly forbidden my Marshall Law), and then cleaning the school area as punishment, happy for being allowed to stay and continue our education, unlike a form in Warsaw, under identical circumstances.

Three months after my finding about Rebecca's soldier boyfriend, between the written and oral parts of the final exams, followed by my setting off for a three-days' voluntary railway exile, and sending her unwritten postcards from different towns of north/east Poland, with photos of streets and market squares named 'Freedom' or 'Liberty'.

Two months after the final exams at the end of my four-years' secondary comprehensive education and my 'sabbat(h)ical' week in a holiday chalet in Gawrych Ruda, right after the orals – seven long nights of drinking loads of beer, sitting at open fire and staring blankly into its flames, with a blanket carelessly thrown over my back, playing some hopeless improvisations on my little harmonica, getting pissed, and having a piss every half an hour (standard beer procedure).

*

August 1982 was hot. I, Ursula and Amanda were staying for two weeks in another chalet in Gawrych Ruda. About a kilometre away from the 'sabbat(h)ical' one. Swimming in Wigry lake and lying on a jetty, sunbathing, for hours. I enjoyed reaching for a package of cigarettes after a swim. Giving Amanda one. Watching drops of water dribble down her wet fringe when she was leaning to get the light. From my lighter. And gazing at me coquettishly with her brown, glistening eyes.

After a few days of exposure to intensive sunshine, Amanda's long brown hair turned fair and she look almost like a peroxide blonde. Ursula's and mine was as if bleached too. The three of us had beautifully, milk-chocolate suntanned, young, strong bodies...

Since there was no grocer's in Gawrych Ruda, every afternoon we walked about three miles to Płociczno, to buy ten bottles of beer. Eight were for me and two for Amanda. We drank it in the evening, sitting at the campfire and singing some stupid songs to my guitar accompaniment.

At the last weekend of our 'Eden' time, on Saturday afternoon, my parents came to stay in the chalet for the night. So, we had to put up a tent nearby, for me, Ursula and Amanda to sleep in. We had purchased the 'provisions' in the morning. Fifteen bottles of beer this time. To celebrate the farewell night. We had hidden all of them in the bushes.

*

When my parents went to bed, I and Amanda said good night to Ursula, who stayed in the tent, we took the bags with the fifteen bottles of beer, and walked to the bridge over the tiny water-link between Wigry lake with Długie Wigierskie lake. About six hundred yards away. Having descended under the bridge, we sat on two big stones, protruding from the water surface, and started drinking the beers, smoking and talking...

I don't know whether it was more beer than before or the fact that it was our last night together, probably forever, but somewhere in the middle of the 'party', we started kissing. At first, it was quite innocent. Our lips me for a few seconds now and then. But with every bottle, the kissing was going wilder and wilder. Including the French stuff...

We were all over each other. Totally out of control. Kissing outrageously. Fondling, caressing, petting. Everything. No, not everything, actually. Although Amanda didn't object to my tongue's penetrating behind her sweet, juicy lips, and my palms squeezing her firm, fair-sized, bra-free breast, and crumpling her full buttocks – she was consequently impeding all my attempts to take her jeans off...

*

Finally, we stood up and started walking towards the chalet. Hand in hand. Taking 'long-cuts'. Across the meadows. Trying to cool down but still kissing and caressing all the way back to the tent.

The following morning, I felt grateful to Amanda for not letting me 'finalize the deal' with her. Regardless of whether it was too little beer, reserves of her drunk decency, fear of her mother's anger, resolution to spare her virginity for future husband, or just bad timing: fertile days or period.

Then Amanda came to Soovowkey once or twice in autumn. And it was nice to have a smoke with her in the playground again. But she kept looking away. And there was no encouragement in her eyes any more. I realized that reaching for my cousin's innocence had been one 'bridge' too far...

*

Chapter 18

Christopher, Marius & Mark

One early June morning 1980, instead of going to school, I and my three form mates bought four large bottles of cheap Polish fruit wine: 'Wigraszek', and went by bus to Płociczno. We walked to Gawrych Ruda and sat on the same old jetty.

We didn't need a corkscrew. The bottle stopper had been eaten away from the inside by sulphur: major ingredient of that 'elegant' beverage. A quick jab-and-pull of the knife point and it was picked out. Piece of cake.

We were drinking the 'wine', trying not to breathe in its poisonous vapour. Swallowing quickly to take our gullies by surprise. And recollecting old good years...

*

One late October afternoon 1979, after the lessons, I, Christopher, Marius and Mark were walking past Soovowkey Town Hall. A historical building about eighty yards from our school. Suddenly, we heard a series of loud whams above our heads and did the runner instantly. A second later I saw two heavy window leaves up in the air. Approaching us. Diving like fighter aircrafts.

I crouched at the last moment. The Messerschmitts missed me and levelled out two yards above the ground to aim at my friends. They were losing their feet for a moment and barely escaped death by throwing themselves flat to the ground. The fighters passed their heads by an inch and crashed right behind them, with a deafening roar of breaking kilograms of glass.

The wind must have broken the window leaves off the old frames on the top storey of the Town Hall. That's what came up with getting a grip over beers at nearby 'Town Hall Café': our Mecca during the long break at school. A pint or two al(l)ways helped us survive subsequent lessons with more dignity.

*

On another occasion, feeling a bit bored with alcohol, we decided to experiment with something else. Something to turn us really on. Speed was not available in early 1980s' Soovowkey. But Christopher remembered that a friend of his, who'd been in prison for a couple years, once mentioned a drink called 'chai'. Very popular in Polish detention facilities then. Convicts used it a lot to brighten up their boring lives. 'Chai' turned out to be nothing else but an exotic name for very strong brew. So, I bought a large package of tea leaves and put the kettle on...

We met on the park opposite our school. I looked around and produced from my bosom a litre bottle full of... tea. First, we got a bit startled by the colour of the drink: vivid, almost fluorescent orange. It didn't look like tea at all. Neither did it taste so.

Each of us took a gulp from the bottle. Fought hard to keep the extremely strong brew inside. Succeeded miraculously. Then we just threw away the half-empty bottle and went for the school disco. To 'dance'.

Soon our pulses became irregular and rapid. Probably two hundred heartbeats per minute. We were 'dancing' for half an hour. Basically, jumping around and screaming. Frightening our neatness freak schoolmates. But soon I started to feel sick and finally the theine overdose swept me off the dance floor. I ended awaken all night. Staring blankly at the ceiling above my bed. Sleepless in Soovowkey...

*

The four of us were fans of hard rock music. Especially Deep Purple and Led Zeppelin. Only Mark preferred Queen. It took us about a year to stop mocking his taste and appreciate more sophisticated rock music as well.

I, Christopher and Marius had a band. It was called Railway Club. From the name of the place where we rehearsed. I played the base and sang. Christopher was the drummer. And Marius played the guitar. He was actually a very good, left-handed guitarist. We played mostly Deep Purple's songs. For about a year...

*

We finished drinking the 'wine' and couldn't stand up. The combination of alcohol, sulphur and hot weather didn't let us. We fought. And we failed. A lot. And coming back to the bus stop in Płociczno turned into our personal 'via dolorosa'.

We were creeping along the asphalt road on all fours. Throwing up every two hundred yards. On the shoulder. Of the road. Mostly. Four 17-year-old students of the best secondary comprehensive school in town. If our teachers could see us then...

After about three hours, we finally managed to get to the bus stop. I reached home. Sat on my bed. And just passed out. When my parents came back from work, they were very worried to see me as pale as the wall behind me.
But my 'I must have eaten something' was enough to calm them down.

My parents didn't know about any of my bad habits. They never noticed little shortages of vodka in my father's drinks cabinet supplies. And they took for granted my poor explanations of alcohol-related poisonings.

That evening I could see two giant shadows on the wall again. Trembling. Moving gently. I could hear soothing sounds. The two magical figures were whispering Love and Devotion. My guardians. Caring.

And I felt so small and broken... Dismantled really... Into pieces... In slow motion...

*

Chapter 19

Files

I parked the car on the road shoulder, walked down under the bridge, and sat on one of the big stones protruding from the water surface. I closed my eyes and entered the universe of a quark. One of its countless streaks of light hosted the combined library & laboratory, where I reached for the file named: 'August 1982 – Gawrych Ruda – Amanda'. I felt through all its contents for a few long minutes...

*

Until my mind became corrupted with everyday routine and unnecessary experience, the archives had been so easy to access. And all files neatly arranged. Perfect order.

*

'December 1973 – Soovowkey – Juliet'. Her green smiling eyes and round and disturbingly protruding buttocks, which bag her checked, tricolour (black, russet and white) linen trousers when she creeps under the bed to fetch something. My reaching under the Christmas tree – the magic still working...

(...)

'June 1974 – Sztabin – Samantha'. Gypsy eyes. Sparkling with smartness. Playful and flirtatious. Behind her black, short hair...

(...)

'December 1975 – Soovowkey – my cousins'. Listening to my stories. I don't know how it works. Ideas coming out of the blue. Some most extraordinary and bizarre plots. My audience amazed. Or bursting with laughter. Clapping their hands. Excited...

(...)

'July 1976 – Marcinkowice – Katherine & Inez'. I am on a summer camp in the mountains. Fall in love with a German girl. Her name's Katherine. But she loves my roommate. While another German girl, Inez, is in love with me. But I'm not bothered. I spend most of the time, sitting on a top branch of the tallest tree in the area, eating candies from the bag in my pocket, and watching the small, boring world below...

(...)

'April 1977' – Jaminy – Karen'. She still breaks my heart with every look in her eyes and every move of her body...

(...)

'August 1978 – Warsaw – Juliet'...

(...)

'July 1980 – Mielno'. I love the sea. Although we have too much rain this season. I'm a sea son. There's a little bar next to our camping site. I dream of coming back in autumn. Without my parents. To drink a few pints there and find love of my life...

(...)

'August 1981 – Swoboda'. Large camping site on Studzieniczne lake shore. Sleeping in tents. Angling. Swimming. Eating delicious dumplings with blue berries. Poured over with sweet cream. We picked up the berries an hour earlier in the primeval forest, which overgrows the lake shoreline...

(...)

'July 1983 – Dźwirzyno'. Another seaside resort. I meet Sylvia. Juliet's cousin. We spend wonderful time together. Maggie Reilly sings *Moonlight Shadow*. Life is beautiful. I and Sylvia fall for each other. The nights so starry. And her kisses make me fly high. Juliet watching us with a mysterious smile. Why her warm green eyes so sad...?

(...)

'August 1984 – Bulgaria'. I and my family enjoy the beautiful climate and scenery of the Black Sea. For the first time. I got completely blotto with Bulgarian wine during a picnic in the mountains. My parents can't believe it. They have never seen me like this before. Start to worry. The sea water is too warm to cool down properly. And too salty to drown. I swim and sunbathe naked. The stretch out on the rocks. All by myself. Once I go to a nudists' beach. Bury erection in the soft sand. My buttocks are not used to so much sunshine. Have to sleep on my stomach for a few nights...

(...)

'July 1985 – Little Geese'. For the first time...

(...)

'March 1986 – Borki'. A training for professional Rebirthers. I meet Maggie...

*

Time passes
Bringing His daughter
Change
Letting Law of Cause and Effect
Apply
God in action
Love

*

Chapter 20

Unnecessary Experience

Since my parents came home late, I and my sister ate dinners in canteens. One rainy day of autumn 1975, I was having bean soup in the basement of Soovowkey Province Government Office, where my father headed their finance department.

Suddenly, a deafening, high-peak noise rose in the corner of the canteen. It was a wheezing, incredible sound. Totally out of this world. I turned and saw that man. He was howling at the top of his voice, shaking all over his body. His face swollen unnaturally. Red and turning purple. All other diners were staring at him. Petrified.

Then the man fell on the floor, into the puddle of his soup and pieces of the plate he had knocked over a moment before jumping to his feet at the start of the attack. His body was shaking more and more violently. Splashing the soup. Now mixed with foam leaking out from his mouth. Someone put a piece of cloth between his clenching teeth

I tottered out of the place and climbed the stairs holding on to the banister. Heavily. I had never seen an epileptic seizure before. I had not realized that a human brain could get so fucked up. I had believed we were all God's children, created in His own image.

Yes, I think that was the time when I stop smiling in that... innocent way... for ever...

*

In early winter 1980, the year of the Gawrych Ruda's 'via dolorosa', I lent my headphones to Christopher. When I started missing my night's music sessions, I asked him to give them back. He told me he had left them at his friend's, who was living in my housing estate. We agreed to meet there.

When I turned up, Christopher was already there, sitting on the sofa, next to his friend, in the latter's small bedroom. They were both looking at me provocatively, beaming. The other bloke, who turned out to be the 'chai' guy, was playing with my headphones...

'Do you want them?', he asked sharply, glaring right into my eyes.
'Yes', I replied uncertainly, looking at Christopher.
'You won't get them,' he concluded aggressively.
'Well... tough luck!', I didn't know what to say.

They both found it hilarious, and started rolling on the sofa laughing (ROTSL). I slammed the door and left. Their amused voices, mocking my awkward response, were chasing my all the way home. And longer. I lost so much that evening. My headphones. My pride. My courage, which betrayed me in the confrontation with the jailbird (a fucking gang rapist). But worst of all... my best friend.

My life was not the same after that experience...

*

I got up around noon at my friend's studer
Warsaw, with a dreadful hangover But it v
bad as the total blank my mind was every
tried to recall any details of the previous night's
party. Nothing. A freaking black hole. It had never
happened before...

It was beautiful spring of 1984 in Warsaw's
Yelonkey: a housing estate for university students. I
stayed there for three years altogether. It's a complex
of wooden houses, built and then inhabited in 1950s
by the Soviet workers employed at construction of
Palace of Culture. 'St. Joseph's Church', as we
sometimes called. Green Yelonkey was located on the
outskirts of Vola, an industrial district of our capital,
nearly 40-minutes' bus ride from the city centre.

Before that first blotto night in my life, I had been
drinking every night for weeks with my friends from
Warsaw Music University. Sometimes, we would
push their wheeled piano along the estate alleys,
playing it loudly and singing our heads off all night
through. But would remember everything the
following morning.

Now, with that heavy head buried in my shaking
hands, I was listening to my friends telling me, with
slightly embarrassed smiles on their faces, how I had
been running around the place, half-naked, waving
my bare member at female-students.

And I couldn't remember a thing. How come? I didn't
understand. Drinking had always been fun. Well...
most of the time... What had happened to me? Had I
gone completely mad?

*

My best friend in Yelonkey was Cauliflower. He'd been nicknamed at a rock festival years before because of that funny style his long, curly hair ruffled in when he crept out of his tent one morning. Good weed often brought good ideas.

Cauliflower wasn't a student. He had left his home town to avoid serving in army and was hiding in student hostels. Year after year. A typical hippie. And a Polish-heroin addict.

In the first year of our friendship he was strong. Sticking to beer and vodka, which we drank together almost every day and night. Of(f) course, we smoked loads of pot too, but it was poor quality stuff. Grown in Poland from secondary seeds. We did laugh after a few joints though. Not sure if it was weed or just sense of helplessness and disappointment with our smoking this shit for hours and feeling so little.

*

Only once in my lifetime did I have a chance to smoke proper stuff: Colombian pot. It was autumn 1983. The beginning of my university studies in Warsaw. One of my year-mates, a beautiful girl, with big blue eyes and very long straight fair hair, got a letter from her friend, who was travelling across South America. Apart from the letter, the envelope contained something that looked like ground tobacco leaves. She knew what it was, and being already aware of my 'interests', gave it to me willingly.

When I rolled a joint and smoked it all alone in my room in Yelonkey, first I didn't feel anything. So, I decided to go to the Old Town to have some wine. On the bus, something strange started going on in my lungs. It was like a thick, heavy and warm wave moving slowly up and down my chest.

I got pretty frightened as I had never experienced anything like that before But then the warmth became very pleasant and started distributing itself all over my body. Making it relax and surrender totally to the effect of the new 'bridge'. My mind felt as if it were reaching Soul again... Touching Her... 'Licking the Heavens'... In slow motion...

When I got off the bus I felt light as feather. Blessed. I walked down the narrow streets of the Old Town, smiling at people. The houses looked quite authentic, as if the whole city hadn't been destroyed completely by the Nazis and rebuilt after the war. I entered the market square, where I often played the guitar and sang, instead of going to classes, to earn some money for a few glasses of 'red, red wine' at nearby Fukier's tavern. I gave up the idea of having one now. I was too high.

When it started getting dark, Time turned back. And I noticed that passers-by were wearing eighteenth century's robes and talking funny. I looked around nervously, and had to sit down on some stairs to think, absolutely amazed by the whole situation. The vision was so real. I could actually touch and talk to people who had been dead for two hundred years. But I didn't. Scared.

It must have lasted quiet a long time, and I was so happy to see a denim jacket finally. A girl was leaning over. I was still sitting on the stairs hiding my face in the hands. She asked if everything was all right. It was. Eventually.

'Some fucking "bridge"', I thought, struggling to my feet, and walked to the bus stop. Quickening the pace.

*

Chapter 21

Cauliflower

Spring 1984 was beautiful. I and Cauliflower began every sunny day by sitting on the lawn in front of my student house and drinking beer. My guitar was always with me. Cauliflower adored my music.

I was often invited to parties and requested to play and sing. I always performed with my eyes closed, as I needed to 'switch off' from reality, to let my mind reach Soul over one of the proper bridges: music. And only when I opened my eyes, having finished a song, could I see that girls looking at me with something more than just interest in my music...

Unfortunately, at the turn of April and May, when Cauliflower scented that poppy flowering season was about to begin, he couldn't stand it anymore and left, promising to be back in October. Soon I had my first blotto experience, following those unforgettable all-night-long open-air piano-playing and singing sessions.

*

Cauliflower kept his word and was back in Yelonkey after summer holidays. Actually, only half of him returned. I didn't ask what had happened to the other half. I knew...

We started drinking together again. But for the first month he got pissed too easily on just a few beers. He would gaze at me sadly. With absent eyes. Asking for his favourite song of mine: 'Piridine Bases'. He kind of liked to hear about the lyrical subject's feeling so down and detached, and longing for his 'high resurrection'.

(YouTube: Ma.Ste. Zasady pirydynowe)

*

Autumn and winter 1984 was probably the worst time of my life ever. Once a month, when I came back to Yelonkey after another weekend in Soovowkey, the money I had from my father to live on for whole month was spent on debts and booze that very night of my arrival.

If Cauliflower and I wanted to drink we had either to borrow money or to take the guitar and walk around the students' housing estate to spot a room where somebody was partying. Then we set down in the corridor I started playing and singing. We always were invited in after a few minutes. And soon our hosts got short of vodka...

I stopped caring about the lapses of mind. It didn't matter anymore that I had been partying all night and could remember only the first couple of hours: the first litre of vodka in my throat. I was down and broken most of Time...

I rarely turned up at the university. Usually when I needed a few days' break from drinking. Motivated by Cauliflower, who was al(l)ways a true friend. Worried about my education.

At classes or lectures I would find myself da[...]
confused. Everything was too normal there. [...]
much to the point. The light was too bright. The li[...]
too straight. I needed a distort to feel more
comfortable. Since acid was not available, I took
headache pills instead. Each with a little cross
carved on its averse and reverse. Dozens of them was
enough to experience altered states. Mostly achieved
by auto-suggestion. But finally I was able to smile at
my year-mates while we were smoking cigarettes at
breaks between classes.

*

As I used to wash the 'crossed' headache pills'
overdose down with loads of soft drinks, my
schoolbag was al(l)ways full of glass bottles. And
every time I rose from my seat at the end of classes
or lectures, the bottles were clinking loudly. Both the
lecturers and other students smiled or laughed at
the sound, assuming that my bag contained the
obvious 'provisions' for another students' party. They
knew I was a rare guest at the university and
imagined how eventful my life must have been
instead. Only my three girlfriends in the group didn't
share the amusement. I often spotted sadness in
their beautiful eyes...

*

In the beginning of winter 1984, Cauliflower gave in.
There was no poppy juice available at that time of
the year. But together with George and Dorothy, the
latter's fiancé, he managed to buy some poppy straw,
acetone, solvent and other necessary ingredients.
Soon they started the production in my room. I
remember watching them sit on the floor in silence
around a metal pot on my small gas stove.

Cauliflower stirred the muddy, boiling liquid with a spoon.

'They look like Indian shamans', I thought to myself, lying on my bed with Jean Paul Sartre's *No Exit* in my hand. Or was it Albert Camus's *The Plague*? The three 'Indians' were long-haired and looked as hypnotised by the ritual. And Dorothy was a witch...

One moony night we went for a walk after my performance at one of the wildest parties a couple of months before. Suddenly, she pulled me to a dark spot. Far from the alley lamps. She lay on the grass and waved at me invitingly.

Beautiful, blue-eyed, fair-haired creature.... But having felt her weak body, far too soft, with most muscles already consumed by hard drugs, I just stroked her head affectionately, fighting back tears, and muttered something about George being my friend and her his fiancé... About not hurting his feelings...

*

I was glad they finally finished. The 'production' didn't bother me, but my house-mates began to complain about the nasty smell of acetone and solvent.

The shamans filled their syringes with the brownish substance, called 'Polish heroin'. The metal pot was empty. Dorothy rolled up her checked, flannel shirt sleeve. Baring the thin, pricked forearm. George helped her gird the left arm above the elbow with a cable. After clenching and straightening her fingers a few times, quickly and skilfully, she injected the whole contents of the syringe slowly into the forearm veins.

They looked at her to see if she was alright. Then George reached out for his fix and treated himself with it accordingly. There was a bit of a problem with Cauliflower, who followed them a minute later. Right after he gave himself the injection, he grew very pale. Dorothy and George had to stand him on his feet against the wall, until his face got back to natural colour. Eventually, he smiled, saying something like 'good stuff', or just 'shivers...'

I observed their pupils. They were narrow as pinheads. I wondered what it would be like to walk over that 'bridge'. How close were their minds to Souls every time they closed their eyes for a long while, smiling...? But somewhere deep inside, I felt it was not a real bridge. I noted my present disillusions with alcohol, which had been supposed to bring me closer to 'Big Answers'. To 'Ultimate Truths'. I realized that even if I had already heard 'Secrets of Being' one night or another I couldn't remember anything. Total blotto...

Yet, I kept drinking heavily, as if asking for a lesson. And the lesson came...

*

Winter 1984 was long and cold. And we were short of cash. People stopped lending us money and inviting to parties. And we had to drink. One very 'dry' day, I went to the local supermarket, took a basket, loaded it with beers, walked behind the shelves to the farthest corner, put most of the bottles into my big, navy-blue schoolbag, hanging on my arm, zipped it up, walked to the cash desk, getting some bread and butter on the way, paid for the contents of the basket, and returned to my room with a dozen bottles of beer I hadn't paid for...

From then on, I went 'shopping' two or three times a day. Not feeling guilty at all. I hated the Communist system and believed that my little 'sabotage' couldn't do more harm to the country than the existing 'science fiction' model of its economy.

One February evening, after all day's drinking beer and vodka, I regained consciousness standing in the supermarket, looking at the broken strap of my schoolbag in the puddle of beer on the floor, and screaming some nasty words into the manager's face. He called the Militia and I spent next 48 hours lying on a 'grand piano', as they called the big wooden box for detainees to sleep on...

The strap of my navy-blue schoolbag had got tangled in the gearwheels of Law of Cause and Effect. And just broke...

When I was arrested, Cauliflower rang up my father, who came to Warsaw the following day. His old friend, with whom he had been studying at the Main School of Planning and Statistics in Warsaw, was now a PhD at the same school. Actually, he lived with his wife and only daughter in a nice house in Yelonkey. They managed somehow to rescue me from three-years' imprisonment for abusive behaviour and assault.

When I saw that look in my father's sad eyes in the morning of my release, and when I recalled then how he had walked me to Soovowkey's bus station once a month, before four a.m., how he had given me the money, saved with so much effort, and the big, warm farewell hugs – my Heart sank...

*

Soon I was summoned to appear in court again, where I was fined for shoplifting and decided to take dean's leave and earn the money to avoid exposing my parents to any further expenses regarding that case. Cauliflower declared his readiness to help and the following week we both found temporal employment at the glassworks in nearby Ożarów.

After three months of carrying bags full of quartz, I had the required amount, paid the fine, thanked Cauliflower, who was already getting ready for the new poppy flowering season, promised to see him again in October, and took a bus to Soovowkey.

*

Chapter 22

Teresa & Natasha

Teresa was living in the opposite student house at Yelonkey estate. She was rather short. Had long dark hair and amazing brown eyes. Wore hippie clothes. Lots of beads and stuff. I sometimes slipped out from another wild party to admire candle lights reflected in her eyes smiling at me through clouds of joss stick smoke.

In spring 1985 I was nearly twenty two and still a virgin. My 'climbing in circles' had developed into proper masturbation about ten years before. Soon I became such a devoted apprentice of that new 'discipline' that Portnoy himself wouldn't complain. I never tried to aim at anything though. Too focused on walking over that 'bridge' inside the universe of a quark in my mind.

I noticed that sensual pleasure of masturbation was more powerful when I smoked a cigarette all through. Nicotine intensified the sensation by triggering new streaks of light inside the quark. Especially during orgasm.

I even tried smoking while making love. But only once. That was with a German girl in the 'sabbat(h)ical' holiday chalet in Gawrych Ruda. She was great. Full-shaped. Long-haired. Big-eyed.

Although we were totally pissed, I think I did manage to make her come somehow. Unfortunately, I failed to get any pleasure from that being too busy to keep the glowing fag away from her sun-dried hair.

*

Apparently, my desire to have a true sexual intercourse at last was a bit weakened then by both excessive, 'nicotinic' masturbation and alcohol abuse. Therefore, when Teresa got down to a blowjob one evening, I felt very excited of(f) course, but not too enthusiastic about it. Especially when she bit on the tip of my penis all of a sudden. I made her stop gently, suggesting that perhaps we should first get to know each other better...

One day, my father's friend, the one who had helped me out of jail, asked if I would be interested in staying in his house for a few days. He, his wife and daughter were going to visit their family, living in my home area, by the way. We didn't know then that ten years later the couple would hit a lorry and get killed on Warsaw-Soovowkey 'road of death': far too narrow for thousands of lorries a day. Their only daughter was orphaned in a spit second.

I and Teresa 'moved in' the following day and I hoped to finally 'become a man'. I played the piano downstairs, than we had a ride on the swing in the garden, ate supper and went to that huge double bed upstairs. Either I felt too nervous or the bite scar was too fresh but... I couldn't do it. We tried later that night and the following nights and... nothing.

I wasn't ready. She was not the one. Maybe too hot for me. And, as a matter of fact, I didn't treat sexual intercourse as a sport activity. Despite what I'd been telling Teresa...

*

Red-haired Natasha's big green eyes were absolutely hypnotizing. Black magic. Pure evil. So tempting, when the witch was creeping towards me on my bed... Despite her alleged disappointment with my sexual 'dysfunction', we got on pretty well. Talking, drinking, smoking and kissing passionately. Until I met Martha...

*

Chapter 23

Martha

When I finished playing the guitar and singing at a party one autumn night of 1985, I noticed that cute girl, who was fixing me with her piercing gaze. Slim, with dark, shortcut hair and black, sparkling eyes. Smiling and raising her glass half-filled with vodka. I reached for mine and we drank together, devouring each other with eyes...

My relationship with Martha was definitely my hitherto most serious. We were living in the same room, sleeping in one bed, smoking, drinking and even eating together, going for long walks or to the opera. Yes, we loved opera, which total opposite of grey 1980s Polish late Communist reality. We did a lot of things together except for one. Making love.

Once she told me about that 'fan club' founded by some of her female friends. The 'members' met now and then to discuss my latest music performances, my looks, my voice, my eyes, or how they had been dreaming about me the previous night... I laughed it off. Of(f) course. But in the heart of my hearts... I felt special and grateful for such secret admiration.

One evening, when I and Martha were lying in bed and kissing, Ann's roommate sped in and screamed madly that she would kill me for what I had done to her friend. When we finally managed to calm her down, she explained that Natasha had got drunk and tried to slash her wrists because of my leaving her...

*

Martha started finding it a bit awkward that we hadn't had any proper sex for months. She wasn't a virgin and I didn't know how to tell her that I was... She knew about my past lifestyle but didn't realize that every time I had got drunk and ended up in a girl's bed nothing ever happened. Alcohol al(l)was got the worst out of me. I became a wild, aggressive, bloodthirsty, barbaric warrior. But no lover.

In January 1986 Martha got sick and went to her parents' to recover. A few days later, I had too much vodka with Cauliflower again. After months of good behaviour. I woke up in a she-neighbour's bed the following morning. Not remembering a thing. Of(f) course, it was very doubtful that I had banged that modest girl the previous night. But Martha's best friend, who just walk in, must have thought otherwise, as she was standing there frozen and staring at me with unspeakable contempt...

A few hours later I was on the train. With my half-empty rucksack and inevitable guitar. Heading south and cursing Graham Bell in my galloping thoughts...

*

Martha greeted me with a sharp look in her 'icebound' black eyes... I was trying to explain that nothing had ever happened. But she only said, three or four times in two days of my stay, that she just wanted me to leave...

All the way back to Warsaw and then up to Soovowkey I was standing in the corridor of the crawling train, jolting up and down, failing to fix my feet on the floor, and staring into the gap between the ajar door and the metal steps of the carriage. The gap was temptingly growing...

I retreated into the filthy, railway (in)convenience and...

'I fixed a dull gaze on the mirror
Wobbly and ownerless my walk
The train swinging with a whisper
Listen you only push the door...'

(YouTube: Ma.Ste. Drzwi)

*

...

*

Chapter 24

London

'So you didn't find the treasure, did you?', She asks sadly.
'No, I didn't'. Tears welling in my eyes...

Old good London. Maggie and I are sitting in Bella Italia restaurant, at 55 Queensway, looking through the menus. The restaurant is busy as always. Now and then swarthy-faced chefs scream humorously in Italian at olive-skinned waitresses to hurry up.

I started coming to this magnificent city in 1991 as export/import manager of a children wear manufacturer. I was a fresh graduate who, already bored with teaching English in one of Soovowkey's secondary comprehensive schools, had welcomed gladly that new opportunity of doing something else for a change. And for better money, of(f) course.

My job was to source clients on UK markets. I travelled to London nearly once a month and met people from Mothercare, Children's World, Adam's Childrenswear, and so on. Soon I gained the status of a regular guest at The Hilton Plaza-on-Hyde-Park Hotel in Lancaster Gate, off Bayswater Road. Jogging in Kensington Gardens every morning was nice.

When I started my own business in 1994, having quitted the position of Office Director of Soovowkey Chamber of Commerce, a few months after my return from Japan, I wanted to become a millionaire overnight. I tried to sell tanks, aircrafts, scandium, osmium, gold, diamonds and other stuff all those different 'bubble-blowers' were offering to me, promising quick and big profit.

Once I even brought a sample of 'Red Mercury' to UK. Or at least a few grams of some red/brownish, thick liquid my cousin had got from a group of Russians and Lithuanians, who claimed it was definitely it. One gram of that substance, if it was real, allegedly cost several thousand US dollars. And we were supposed to be able to supply kilograms per month.

Of(f) course, I and my cousin never found out if our 'preciousssss' material was worth anything at all. Our prospective 'clients' (probably UK secret service) failed to come back to us at all after that appointment we had had with them in a posh restaurant. So, we had to return the sample to the Russian/Lithuanian group (probably mafia).

*

On another occasion, in 1995, I was staying in the The Hilton Plaza-on-Hyde-Park Hotel for two weeks: one waiting in vain for a buyer's decision and the other trying to raise funds to pay the room bill. That was the week when I got grey at the sides... At the age of 32... So it was not only genes...

I finally managed to borrow the fifteen hundred quid from my friend. A decent, elderly Englishmen and a former client of my former employer. Then a former friend of mine as well...

I have a few good friends, who are also my business associates, in different parts of UK. There is Robert in the south – once a billionaire, with a set of luxurious cars, including two Rolls-Royces, then conned by his own accountant. Roger in London – scolding one of his solicitors, screaming with glottal-stopped cockney to the mobile: 'Don't try to nikky me, you plonka!', and driving away in his convertible Porsche. Or Michael in the north – one of my best friends ever, who deserves a separate book to be written about or by him.

*

'I appreciate your response to my complaining about "forced migration", She tries to cheer me up. Puts the menu away. All stars sparkling in Her green eyes. 'But what do you mean by saying that "absolute knowledge" is a contradiction of terms?'
'Well, that's obvious, isn't it?', I don't ask. 'Absolute is beyond any knowledge. Knowledge is just an outcome of relativity...'
'And wisdom?'
'Wisdom is the ability to make good choices in life.'
'Hmm... Right...'
'But don't you have any other comments on the preceding passages? Didn't you like the chronology in my description of the process of "feeling through files in combined library & laboratory"?'
'Yes, I thought for a while that you were writing a diary. And have you noticed that "file" is an anagram of "life"? Every memory, feeling, emotion, thought and idea is actually "living" in your head.'

'There must be something in it. I translate lots of birth, school, employment, marriage, divorce and death certificates. My hard disc is "heavy" with files. And every such file is a life too. Or at least a formal testimony to a crucial event in someone's existence. My clients bring their lives to my office.'

'Anyway, I managed to swallow the... "pill" of hard times in your life somehow. Still "digesting" it probably. And either the "pill" hasn't started working yet or it's just a... "placebo"!' She burst out laughing. 'I forgot there had been so many girls in your life before you finally met me... I mean, Maggie...'

'There was another one, actually. My secondary comprehensive school form-mate. Mary had hardly noticed me during our secondary school education. But then we met again, few years later, in Gawrych Ruda. Not far from the "sabbat(h)ical" holiday chalet. Her family, who were staying there one summer made a large open fire and invited me with my inevitable guitar. She couldn't tear her gaze away from me, when I was playing and singing all night long. Oddly enough, I drank so much then and yet didn't go blotto. At dawn, the two of us decided to go angling. We were both pissed enough to start kissing. We laid on green grass of Wigry lakeshore by the same old jetty. I was stroking her naked tummy and trying to lower my fingers under her white, little (sssss)sexy (sssss)knickers. But she didn't let me... in. Smiling instead. Saying we were too drunk. Promising to meet me later today. Then she stood up and walked slowly to her family holiday chalet, away on the hill behind the spruce trees... And I fell asleep on the jetty, with the fishing rod in my hand, dreaming of some Vikings, who moored their ancient ship to the nearby pier and invited me to an exciting cruise in the north seas...'

'So many girls and no proper fuck!', She laughed again. 'If I didn't know about your waiting for love of your life: Maggie, I would suspect that there was something wrong with you...'

'No, I didn't have any problems with erection. Masturbating several times a day...'

'Yeah, I remember. With a fag in your mouth. But I mean, something wrong with your... 'preferences', you know...'

'Oh no, I have never in my life had any homosexual inclinations. Never. Of(f) course, as you know, I like gays very much. Especially lesbians. But I don't like when they make a show of their alternative sexuality. Even if it's in self-defence. I don't like when they claim that their otherness is normal. It is not. Just like the "in through the outdoor" stuff is not normal. Either in homo- or in heterosexual intercourses. Unfortunately, God made an anatomical mistake by installing the "garbage dump" too close to the "funfair". Which gets some people confused... Please stop laughing and let me finish... No, it is not normal. But it is not wrong either. We all have free will and are free to exercise it in the given conditioning. Look at me. I'm far from being normal. Yet am I a bad person?'

'And what about that boy you went to handball training with?'

'But he was so girlish...', I say raising my eyebrows in disbelief. 'Of course, I remember him. I started playing in our school handball team, as a left-winger, as the "stability" of the soccer goalkeeper position, combined with my love for sweets, had been pushing me to the chubby side too much. He was from another primary school, but we often met in the gym-room, during many inter-school competitions or trainings. How old could we be then? Twelve? Maybe thirteen.... And he was so girlish... With beautiful, smooth and clean complexion. While my face was coarse and rough as a grater...

I had terrible common acne for too many years...
And during our trainings, I couldn't help watching him closely when he was landing on a pile of exercise mats after a jump. Spreading his hairless, shapely legs... He was slim, shortcut-black-haired and olive-skinned...'

'Can I take your order, sir?', the teenage Italian waitress looks exactly the same as the boy I was just describing to Maggie.

After a moment of awkward staring, I order the usual: a vegetarian pizza. And Maggie, as usual: something unusual...

*

We finish the meal and go for a long walk, taking the route I had a chance to know so well during my numerous visits here. We walk down Bayswater Road. Past Marble Arch. Into Oxford Street. Turning right in Oxford Circus. Along Regent Street to reach Piccadilly Circus. Into Haymarket, on the Circus's other end. Then left, into Pall Mall. Around Trafalgar Square. Down Whitehall. Through Parliament Street. Then right, into Great George Street. Along Birdcage Walk. Across the Fore Court. Down Constitution Hill. Past Wellington's Monument. Into Knightsbridge. Through Kensington Road. Past Royal Albert Hall, where Deep Purple and the Royal Philharmonic Orchestra, conducted by Mr Malcolm Arnold, performed John Lord's 'Concerto for Group and Orchestra' back in September 1969, when I was nearly six. And finally, across Kensington Gardens, past Albert Memorial, along Lancaster Walk, back to the hotel...

'Have you "digested the pill" yet?', I ask somewhere in the middle of our walk.
'Yess. And I think I have a definition of your writing. It's "quasi-literary, hyper-sincere, self-psychoanalytic, spiritual & progressive fiction, with elements of esoteric Gnosticism". And please don't use your "Past Past Past Perfect" or even "Past Past Perfect" tenses any more. They just don't sound right...'

*

'And do you remember the "new style in poetry" I invented years ago?', I look at her, smiling, while we are walking past the reception desk the following morning, to have our breakfast at The Hilton Plaza-on-Hyde-Park Hotel restaurant. The concierge at the entrance greets us with a courtly, yet friendly bow and, knowing me quite well, beams only, sparing the standard question: 'English or continental?'.

Those who don't know the trick, and choose the latter, will get just toasts, jam and coffee. While the English breakfast diners will be having everything: eggs & beckon, sausages and hams, cereals, all possible fruits of the world - fresh, fragrant and juicy – beautiful fruit salads and many kinds of juices...

'Do you mean the "rhythm-free quasi-rhyming"?', She leans towards me.
'Yess. Unfortunately, I composed only one "poem" in this "style"...'
'Yes, it's called "On Marriage", isn't it?' she doesn't ask. 'How was it?' Now she does ask. So, I start 'reciting'. Stressing unnaturally the last syllable in every verse:

'Oh do I love <u>her</u>?
Well, she's night<u>mare</u>...
And I don't mind this status of <u>lien</u>,
as long as she lets me be her night sta<u>llion</u>.'

'Of(f) course, you don't mean that, do you?' She asks again, looking up at me from her plate, a minute later, when we have already brought everything we needed to our table in the corner of the English breakfast room.
'Nah. Marriage as miserable formal arrangement where sex is the only consolation for men? Don't be silly. You know I love you... I mean Maggie... So much... And I always will. Regardless of anything. Including Time and whatever other conditioning... When I think of our relationship I don't focus its "here and now" only. I visualize thousands of years of our being together. We are "Soul-mates". Our Souls are fragments of One and the same Pure Unconditional and Everlasting Love. Naturally, our minds try to understand Soul and God by their own standards and thus we create God in our own image. But since HE/SHE IS (I AM) Absolute, no physically-oriented mind can ever understand HIM/HER. '
'I think you were right to title your books of songs: "B.C." and "A.D." With Maggie at your side, it was the beginning of a new era in your life, wasn't it?'
'True. She saved me. She's my Angel. Although, I made a decision to change my life a little earlier. Two or three weeks after Martha had told me to go, my uncle John, Emily's father, asked me to interpret two UK instructors of Re-birthing, Robin and Ross, at a training course in... Gawrych Ruda. A couple of days later I had my first conscious breathing session there. I was breathing continuously, regularly and deeply for over an hour, under the supervision of another participant of the training, who kept telling me to focus on inhale/exhale unbreakable circle. All the way through I cried a lot. And I laughed a lot.

It was an amazing and extremely powerful experience. Better than masturbation, drugs and alcohol. An (Ab)so(l)u(te)ly True BRIDGE. That was the moment when I chose to start living "upwards", and the following month I met Maggie...'

*

'But the song the first stanza of which you quoted at the end of the description of your "desperado" ride on the train to Soovowkey found itself in "B.C." book of songs, didn't it?' she may ask, when after breakfast, we step out of the lift on the third floor of The Hilton Plaza-on-Hyde-Park Hotel and start walking to our room to pack our stuff before this afternoon's flight from Heathrow Airport back to Poland.
'Yes it did', I answer, looking down on the thick and soft fitted carpet and wondering how they can manage to put all the pieces together to form such a perfect, self-contained whole. 'That song, called "The Door", track 13 on the third album: "Soovowkey calling (1978 – 1987)", never released in 2004, under my "Home Made Music Box" project, was inspired by Ruby Nelson's wonderful book: *The Door of Everything*. As well as by other books and teachings of Re-birthing philosophy. And it had been written shortly BEFORE I met Maggie.'

We enter the room. I sit on the bed and take out my inevitable guitar from the case. And the case is open... When I start playing and singing:

'I fixed a dull gaze on the mirror
Wobbly and ownerless my walk
The train swinging with a whisper
Listen you only push the door

And suddenly a warm hand
Touched my Heart
A Bright Figure
Pervaded me
The New Spirit
Spoke
And the Secret
Is no more to me

You are the almighty ruler of the stars
Death is your servant and so is the Time
Your thoughts set the course of events
You'll bang your head through the wall
If you wish

To you
Cowering in hangover
To you
The victim of your dreams
To you
Wretched of your own free will
To you
Always wanting to take
With no satisfaction

To all
Lost in the gloom of evil
To all
Searching for the daylight
I say you only push the Door
And all God's children
Will be gods again

You are the almighty ruler of the stars
Death is your servant and so is the Time
Your thoughts set the course of events
You'll bang your head through the wall
If you wish'

(YouTube: Ma.Ste. Drzwi)

*

Chapter 25

Two Hearts

'No bid!', says Ursula, putting her cards on the table and reaching for a cookie.
'One heart...', Maggie bids with her magic voice.
'No trumps!', Edward, my brother-in-law, announces convincingly.
'Two hearts...?', I say quietly, looking into my wife's beautiful, green eyes, with hope...

'You know, I'm not sure about the quotations of your lyrics in this book', I can hear it in my head. Her lips smiling only, from the other side of the table. *'When famous singers, like Sting – "S(t)ingers" – make references in their autobiographies to particular pieces of their music, everybody knows what they are writing about. Some would sing along while reading. And it makes perfect sense. While here we've got the lyrics but nobody has ever heard the music. What do you want to achieve?'*

'Well', I reply slowly, learning the telepathic transmission, *'Perhaps it is the mission of this... book. To promote my music. To get prospective readers interested in what it may sound like... And then if this... book were ever going to be published, I could use it in support of my negotiations with some record companies...'*

'You're a dreamer, aren't you?', Maggie doesn't ask aloud. Thus interrupting the direct mind-to-mind connection. Another game of 'bridge'...

*

Chapter 26

Jigsaw Puzzle

I had to wait another five long years after the conscious breathing session in Gawrych Ruda, until Law of Cause and Effect finally started producing expected results of my choice to live consciously and 'upwards'. It was a test of Time...

From October 1986 through June 1987 was the worst. Ten long months of separation from Maggie. She lived in Lodz while I got stuck in Warsaw. After four years of 'studying' there, with two dean's leaves on my scorecard, I was still on the second year. For the third time in a row. I needed those credits badly. My beloved was waiting.

This Time, I was staying in a student hostel in another district of Warsaw: Ohota. I shared the room with a true Peruvian Indian from Lima, Oscar, who taught me how to play the guitar more gently: by strumming the strings. We had a band called 'The Wandering Mountains', and performed quite regularly in the Old Town or at some international music events in different parts of Warsaw. I played main Latino themes on the mandolin, Oscar on the samponia (which sounded like wind blowing across the Andes), and Mark on the charango...

I wish I had been more attentive when Oscar's South American friends living in Poland visited him in our room and talked Spanish all Time. I managed to grasp just a few phrases. I greeted such visitors with a promising 'Siéntate, por favor. ¿Quieres té?', only to disappoint them, after a few seconds of their 'galloping' Spanish, that I could actually speak just Polish, Russian and English.

I had conscious breathing sessions almost every day and only one wild party during the whole academic year, when my sister's ex form-mates, who were also studying in Warsaw, stepped by, one late autumn evening. Oscar was away, and we got drunk and accidentally destroyed his plumage, when playing Indians in the corridor. That was a cheap, fake headdress, which Oscar had been wearing occasionally to cheer up his friends, but the fact that I had taken it from his wardrobe made him go really mad. He was screaming into my face that he didn't understand how someone who declared to be living consciously and 'upwards' could ever got so barbarian.

He was right, for the first five years of Re-birthing, my life was a sequence of 'ups & downs' or 'highs & lows', despite my sincere intentions and declarations. Still it was only 'lip service'... The word wasn't made flesh yet... But I felt I was going in the right direction...

*

In March 1990 I decided to get a grip on myself. I was already on the fifth year of English Philology at Lodz University and married for two and a half years to Maggie, who was now five-months' pregnant. I started fasting every other Monday, shaving my head once a week, jogging, exercising, breathing consciously on daily basis, and writing my M.A. thesis: *A Self-Portrait Of James Joyce As A Young Man* in the meantime. Four months later I was at the top of my mental and physical shape, feeling more and more Light in my life.

However, something was still not right. I couldn't quit smoking. And once a month had to take a break to get drunk and let the demons out...

*

In June my first son was born. I was so happy. And so proud of Maggie. In July we moved to Soovowkey and in September I started teaching English in the secondary comprehensive school.

In 1991, as export/import manager of the children wear manufacturing company, I was too busy to continue my spiritual development, but always managed to find a moment to go for a drink with my employer's clients.

One autumn morning, I woke up in a strange place, with a big black hole in my memory. I rushed to search nervously through the 'files' in the combined library & laboratory and opened the one labelled: 'Last Night'... There was nothing inside... It was all empty... I looked around in panic and finally identified my current location. Soovowkey Detoxification Detention Centre...

The police officer told me a few hours later that previous night I had been driving my car on public road, being in the state of intoxication: 3.4 pro mille of alcohol in my blood. They retained my driving licence for twelve months...

'That's it...', I thought to myself back at home. 'It's now or never!'
And I have not had any alcohol, cigarettes, meat, fish or eggs, in my mouth since then... I learnt that lesson..., eventually!

*

'I think it was meat that kept the alcoholic demons alive, even though mind was already set in the right direction', I say to Maggie on the plane from London. But She doesn't reply. Asleep. With Her head in the halo of beautiful long golden hair. Resting on my shoulder.

I look out of the window to contemplate the clouds (mind) hanging above the Earth (body) and below the sky (Soul) above. I recall the fitted carpet I was walking on with Maggie on the third floor of The Plaza on Hyde Park Hotel
and it occurs to me that all divisions are far-fetched and unnecessary.

If I had perceived myself as perfect, self-contained Oneness, I wouldn't have needed to search for any 'bridges' all my life. Perhaps we cannot understand the simplicity of the structure of the universe and its different dimensions, because we don't give ourselves a chance to look at things from the right perspective, which would allow us to see through the illusory complexity of the world's mosaic, and understand what we call 'irony of fate'.

*

My grandfather died of lung cancer after chain-smoking for fifty years. My father struggled with the same habit for thirty years. I for twenty. And now one of my major clients is... British American Tobacco! I translate all their office and factory procedures and best practices, PMD and SMD machinery manuals. I know everything about flue cured tobacco or strips, reconstituted tobacco, rod weight or firmness corrected, end stability, rod filter PD, tip ventilation, puff number, infestation control, and so on.

Sometimes it seems that two jigsaw puzzle pieces we are holding in our hands at the combined library and laboratory will never match. And a moment later they fit into the puzzle right next to each other. I'm a fan of James Joyce and Syd Barrett but was sure for years they had nothing in common. Until I found out that the lyrics of one of my favourite Barrett's song: 'Golden Hair' (from his first solo album: 'The Madcap Laughs', recorded in May 1968) was actually Joyce's poem V from his *Chamber Music* (his first collection of poems, published in May 1907. So now, every time I play and sing Barrett's best song ever: 'Feel', I close my eyes and dive in the universe of *Ulysses* and *Finnegan's Wake*.

*

Chapter 27

Inroibo ad altare Dei

'Remember how I got pissed at my own wedding reception?', I turn to Maggie, who is resting Her back on the backrest of our light pink and white narrow-stripped coach in our green room.
'Maggie had never seen you drunk before', She looks up at me with her sleepy green eyes. We have just arrived from Warsaw airport after the London trip. It's late at night...
'But you had. And lot. I was just a waste of space. Being me must have been the worst job in the world Soul can ever get. Was that why you stopped talking to me at some point?'
'I'm not your Soul.'
'What?'
'I am not.'
'Say what?'
'I never said I was, did I?'
'What the fuck?!'
'Polease...'
'Who are you then?! Whom have I been talking to all this time?!'
'Did you really think you could talk to your Soul? To God?'
'Neale Donald Walsch does...'

'Then you miss the whole point. Go read his books again. Soul, which is God's element inspiring quark universes in our physical body, belongs to Sphere of Absolute. And Absolute is beyond any knowledge. Beyond any outcome of relativity. You said so yourself. Soul is beyond any words. She doesn't know any words and thus remains speechless. Al(l)ways. Knowledge, surface mind's domain, is too small and primitive to reach and sully Her Absolute Wisdom and Innocence.'

'I know who you are!', I scream from the top of my voice right into her face. 'You are my fucking, sick…, sick and devilish… muse! You al(l)ways make me lose my sanity for the sake of some… fucking art! You distract me from and deprive me of my family life by pushing me into some stupid… projects! Your "inspirations" force me to spend hours, days, weeks, months, years… composing and playing that fucking music, and now writing this… whatever it is… at the cost of my family, business, social and spiritual life! Ruining my poor sight and spine! I hate you! I hate you for my over-sensitivity, sentimentalism and self pity you have brought upon me with your fucking "inspirations"! You "inspired" me to search for "bridges"! And there are no fucking "bridges"!!! You've sucked all my deepest secrets out of me! You have stolen my Soul! Now, if I ever signed anything in the context of this… book, with some fucking publisher, it wouldn't be a contract, but a pact!!!'

I speed out of the room and rush back in, hardly noticing that its walls are glowing red now…

'And you know what! You were right in Sulejówek! I don't love you! I only love my conception of you! I love a girl whom you are not! Never were and never will be! And you don't love me either! You never did! You can't love at all! You cunt!!!

*

The black waters of Wigry lake turn into one huge, treacherous whirlpool, spinning around violently, flooding the shores, with extremely strong current dragging the eels, pulling them down under, deeper and deeper, sucking them in, as if they are being swallowed by some powerful, monstrous drain...!!!

The whole Baltic Sea gives way under madly raging storm, with wildest winds roaring all across, and heavy rain, slanting in all directions!!! The snakes, chased and hit by ruthless thunderbolts, are leaping up high above gigantic waves...!!!

Mount Fuji explodes with fire, spitting boiling lava out of its shaking throat, with thick, grey, ashy clouds enveloping the whole island!!! The ground is shuddering from a terrible earthquake...!!!

I AM FURIOUS!!!

*

I'm following Christopher across the desert dunes of North Africa. Each of us riding powerful Bombardier's 4W ATV. Dressed in dark like hell, leather trousers and zipped up jackets with fringed sleeves we are speeding hot-wheel, at the top of the gear. The dry wind would be playing rough with our hair if we had any. Our heads, bald as coots, are being beaten down by the harsh desert sun. Our eyes, screwed up (mine totally) behind blackest sunglasses, are fixed on the sky-high, yellowish, cloudy wall in front of us. We are the 'riders of the (sand)storm'...

I suddenly rein in my steel steed and dismount from the saddle, waiting for Christopher to see me shrinking in the wing-view of his 'Motor Pegasus'. He turns around to approach me.

'My dear friend', I speak to him in hoarse voice, when he brakes hard an inch from my knee. 'I can't go where you are going. I don't listen to Deep Purple, Rainbow, Led Zeppelin, Uriah Heep or Black Sabbath any more. I prefer Mike Oldfield now. Forgive me. As I forgive you. And... farewell.'
'May the Force be with you, Maste', he replies, smiling ironically.

We shake hands and I start walking west, towards the sunning set...

*

'Denotni dna tfola lwob eht dleh eh. Ria gninrom dlim eht yb mih dniheb-yltneg deniatsus saw, deldrignu, nwog gnisserd wolley a. Dessorc yal rozar a dna rorrim a hciwh no rehtal fo lwob a gniraeb, daehriats eht morf emac nagillum kcub pmulp, yletats.

"Inroibo ad altare Dei."'

*

Chapter 28

Reunion

I'm walking down Noniewicza Street, towards Czarna Hańcza. Having meandered across the hilly, postglacial area of the landscape park in the north, the river cuts through Soovowkey to roll along the winding bed of Wigry lake in the national park in the south. It's one of the most scenic canoeing route in Europe. Truly unmatched beauty of unspoilt nature.

I can see the wooden bridge in front of me. Maggie is sitting on a bench right behind it. On the other bank of the river. At the foot of the hill, overgrown with coniferous wood. I walk over the bridge. The waters are clear, despite the river's name. 'Czarna' means 'black' in Polish.

I sit next to Maggie. I'm pretty tired, actually. It's been hell of a walk from Sahara. But I needed that to cool down. We are sitting in silence, watching the swift waters flow before our eyes...

*

The river is only five to seven metres wide. But in my dream, one of the repetitive dreams I still have, it's always as big as a lake. And the tree trunks on the hill are a few yards' thicker, hidden behind huge fronds of some monstrously-sized ferns...

I swim in the river together with some strangers. We don't know each other but feel familiar. Laughing. Jumping and diving. Totally indifferent to our nakedness. Uninterested in each other's gender. Just enjoying the swim...

Another alternative reality. Maybe inspired by signals from genetic level, which contains information about human life on the banks of Czarna Hańcza River millions years before the fall of man. When our minds had al(l)ways made conscious choices, under 'free will' privilege, to surrender totally to Soul. When we had been aware of being embodiments Pure, Unconditional and Everlasting Love. Happy. For ever young. Enjoying our immortal bodies' participation physical universe.

We had been free from any desires and conditioning, as the Good Shepherd: our Soul, had been taking care of us. We hadn't felt any need for food, drink or shelter. Modern archaeologists will never find any traces of our living on this planet then. Even if they dig very deep in the ground. And we had been riding dinosaurs!

*

But what happened then? Why and how did we fall? Is eating that apple from the tree of knowledge of good and evil a metaphor for the outcome of our minds' 'free will' decision to seek experience on their own? Outside and regardless of Soul. Was it about our choosing individualism and knowledge for the sake of mere curiosity, which at some point became stronger than hitherto surrender and innocence?

Or perhaps the old story should be taken literally? Maybe the fall started with the first bite of the fruit. We found eating enjoyable. The food put our minds to sleep, which we had not known before. Soon, one of us came up with an idea to taste some flesh. And eventually, we all ended up as animals, living in caves, hunting down and eating our less smart brothers... Looking forward to evolution, which would let us make more lethal weapons.

Evolution or revolution, or aliens' landing... Same difference. If considered from vast perspective of the universe of a quark inspired by White Light of Soul. By Pure, Unconditional and Everlasting Love.

*

'I'm sorry,' I break the silence, not looking at Her. 'I must have absorbed past negativity from my recollections...'

'It's OK,' She turns to embrace and kiss me.

*

Chapter 29

Fire @ Will

I'm playing 'Fire @ Will' on the piano in our living room. This instrumental piece of music is the quintessence of all my intuitive composing. It's about human (super)natural power, lying dormant in each of us. Our latent talent to kindle fire of or by our own. Pillar of Fire inside physical body. Burning Bush illuminating mind.

This number found itself as title track on my last album, unreleased in 2007 under Home Made Music project, bearing the same title. The cover is a photo I took in winter that year. It shows my index finger up in the foreground and my beautiful, holy, loner's open fire in the background. The picture's message is clear: 'Let there be fire'.

(YouTube: Ma.Ste. Fire @ Will)

*

It's Sunday noon. My wife and two sons are in church. I am not. But Jesus Christ is my closest Master of Being, both geographically and emotionally.

He's Master of Physical Immortality, who resurrected his physical body and lives all through Time and different dimensions, including physical universe. And it's irrelevant if He's been ever married or not. With or without children.

We are all God's children. All the same beings. Humans with divine potential. Participating in physical dimension. Subject to its relativity: manifestation of Law of Cause and Effect. Blessing and cursing free will with every choice we make to cope with our genetic and contextual conditioning.

Unfortunately, Catholic Church sees is in a different way. Its priests tell us to pray to Jesus. Instead of encouraging us to follow his example. They claim to be intermediaries facilitating our contact with God. As if He were somewhere outside of us. But God is everywhere. Even in churches...

*

It's Monday. The other Monday. I'm with Jerry. He's my father's elder sister's youngest son. We are sitting on the same old jetty. It's all covered with snow now. And we were listening to whales' singing...

Huge slabs of ice-bound waters of Wigry lake move as majestically as tectonic planes. Only faster. And every Time they come into contact with each other, they produce that particular, enchanting sound...

We enjoy the hypnotising concerto of the whales. Their music echoes inside every quark of our physical bodies. Especially in the universes of our brains. Spirit, mind and body have become one (a)gain. Sea snakes are silent. And so are lake eels. Just electricity.

*

An hour later Jerry and I are walking among old trees. Two oaks in front of us are like husband and wife, with his muscular boughs wrapping around her slender trunk, and their crowns caressing each other high up in the wind as if they are kissing... Every time I walk past this couple I imagine them living in human bodies as two beautiful lovers. Here, on Wigry lakeshore. Hundreds years ago...

All trees are our brothers. Jerry gives a lonely tree nearby a big hug. I clasp another one in my arms. We hold on like this for a long while. Our eyes closed. We are breathing deeply. Feeling the oneness with our brothers. Brothers in arms...

Then we start gathering brushwood, choosing small and dry pieces protruding from the snow, and putting them on top of each other carefully. This Time we are building a special fire...

After half-an-hour's work, we are looking at a fair-sized stake. Who are we going to burn? All our negativity, of(f) course...

*

I strike a match and the stake catches the fire. We sit in the semi-Lotus positions. The flames grow and we let them cleanse our Auras and Chakras. The Fire sends us into a trance. We start reciting *Baird T. Spalding's affirmations*:

'Deep inside of me, dwells the Divine Alchemist – the true Love of God, disclosed in the Eternal Youth. In my Spiritual Temple, the Divine Alchemist constantly coins new and beautiful baby cells. The Spirit of Youth within my body is the Human Form Divine, and all in me is always sound, beautiful and young. Within me, there is a perfect form – the form Divine. I am now all that I desire to be I visualize daily my beautiful being until I breathe it into expression. I am a Divine Child, all my needs are now and forever supplied. Infinite Love fills my mind and thrills my body with its perfect life. May Love, Wisdom and Peace flow from me to all humanity. May the whole world and all humanity be happy and blessed.
AUM, AUM, AUM...
PEACE, PEACE, PEACE...
OM NAMAHA SHIVAYA, OM NAMAHA SHIVAYA, OM NAMAHA SHIVAYA!'

The fire flames reach above our heads and all our Chakras spin around magnificently...

'Here and now it becomes real to me that deep inside me there is joyful, Spiritual Body – eternally young and infinitely beautiful. It has wonderful, spiritual mind, beautiful and healthy eyes, nose, lips, ears, teeth and skin. The whole body has harmonious, beautiful, shapely, healthy and young structure. Deep inside me Spirit spreads His wings and fills my Spiritual Body – Divine Temple – with Light. All organs of my body function perfectly and in complete Harmony with each other. Now and always I have perfect body of God's Child.
AUM AUM AUM...
PEACE, PEACE, PEACE...
OM NAMAHA SHIVAYA, OM NAMAHA SHIVAYA, OM NAMAHA SHIVAYA..."

*

Then we uttered magic spells and draw secret symbols in the air, visualising how Golden Rays of Reiki come down from Heavens upon our Crown Chakras and pierce all through our bodies.

*

We mantra chant Violet Fire decrees faster and faster, until they flow out of our Hearts straight into the flames, so swiftly that mind hardly manages to follow...

*

I say my own little prayer:

'Dear God, please, let White Healing Light fill all my mind and all my body throughout this meditation. Dear God, please, let White Healing Light rinse, all evil, all toxins, all negativity, all diseases, all illnesses, all illnesses, all illnesses, out of my mind and out of my body, to flow out, out, out of my palms right into the flames of this fire, all throughout this meditation, leaving my mind and my body for ever, to burn and change miraculously into Divine, Cosmic Energy of Love...'

In course of the prayer I keep wiping all negativity out of my body, by scanning it from the top of my head to the knees. I do it with both my hands. I shake them violently towards the fire, at the end of every cycle, to throw invisible, undesired energy into the flames. Thus burning my 'bad witches' at the stake...

*

Finally, we do the twenty five connected conscious breaths while I recite in my thoughts: 'I breathe in Love and Good" (at the fifth, longest and deepest inhale of the first cycle), 'I breathe in Health, Health, Health' (at the fifth, longest and deepest inhale of the second cycle), 'I breathe in Life, Life, Life' (at the fifth, longest and deepest inhale of the third cycle), 'I breathe in Peace, Harmony and Equilibrium' (at the fifth, longest and deepest inhale of the fourth cycle), 'I breathe in Light, Energy and Strength' (at the fifth, longest and deepest inhale of the fifth cycle).

We sing AUM many times and start proper meditation, clearing our minds off any thoughts whatsoever, leaving there only White Light and AUM sound. We enter the universe of a quark...

*

After meditation, we rake over the living embers, distributing them evenly, and muttering the fire walk mantras...

When it's all set and ready, I stand before the 'magic carpet' of fire. The glowing carpet is fitted with dying out flames. It's all so clear to me now... I see THE BRIDGE... I close my eyes and start walking over it...

I have already been in trance for over two hours. With my eyes closed, I can feel how mind and body surrender totally to Soul. I am integrated. I AM ONE. With every step, my feet welcome the living embers gladly and experience my Whole Being's unity with the element of Fire...

I wait for Jerry to join me on the other side of the FIERY BRIDGE. Then I go back into the flames... (A)gain. And (a)gain. And (a)gain...

If Soul had a mouth, She would smile broadly. Here and now.

*

Chapter 30

Music

All the way home from the fire walk ceremony I sing out loud, driving the car and Jerry crazy...

*

'I don't care
What I do
I just am
Have no fear
Love is here

I don't care
I don't have to
Any more
I am free
Love is here

Fresh green
Against clear blue
Sunshine in your hair
Bright atoms in the air
Dance and sing
The same old song
And I can't help
Singing it to you
Again

Love - high vibrations of the light
Love - magic sparkles in your eyes
Full of promise smile
That I wanna kiss

Sad look
Of tired green
Darkened navy blue
Yet full of twinkling stars
Which dance and sing
The same old song
And I can't help
Singing it to you
Again'

(YouTube: Ma.Ste. Mission Statement)

*

'Time is on our side
Every moment glows
Love light
Reach high heavens
Close your eyes
Peace deep in mind
Let spirit be your guide

Now I see
The world that people call reality
Is just a playground for surface minds
A queer mixture of good and bad
Will not deceive my pure Soul

My pure Soul
Now leads me out
Of this verisimilitude

Higher
We are getting higher
Love defeats desire
And rain with the sun
End up in a rainbow
And no sorrow
To pure joy I surrender

My ego has been flooded
With the starlight of Love
It drifts in calm waters
Of omniscient self
My body now follows
My enlightened mind
And up they all head
In harmonious rise'

(YouTube: Ma.Ste. Good News)

*

'Sounds
And reflections
On the walls
Of crystal palaces
Time
And vast spaces
In my room
Breathe deep
And close your eyes

I get the answer
Prior to a question
When I open up all my mind
Flying into Light
I keep on breathing
Through pain and heavy air
Past burdens and gravity
I leave behind

Approaching weightlessness'

(YouTube: Ma.Ste. Breathing Session)

*

'This way my Love I'll show you how
We can live forever
Always young
Let go your fear – burn down the past
Now be one with everything
Since everything is one

I've been away for many thousand years
Now it's time to come back
Into this light of everlasting love

Maybe I will eat and maybe I will sleep
Maybe I will love and maybe I will stop
It's a river that flows out of my brain

Maybe I will work and maybe I will not
Maybe I will talk and maybe I will walk away
My head's a mess
Save me Lord

Take my thoughts and turn them into Light
I don't need them any more
The way they are
They are waste of space

Take my heart and fill it with pure joy
Make it loving
Make it meek
The way you are
It belongs to you

Maybe I'll be good and maybe I'll be bad
Maybe I will laugh and maybe I'll be sad
There's a fire
There's a wind
But
I don't know

Maybe I will fall and maybe I will fly
Maybe I will live and maybe I will die
I need quiet
I need peace
Save me Lord

Take my thoughts and turn them into Light
I don't need them any more
The way they are
They are waste of space

Take my heart and fill it with pure joy
Make it loving
Make it meek
The way you are
It belongs to you'

(YouTube: Ma.Ste. Here & Now)

*

'I've been waiting
So long
For you
To come

So why don't you
Do it
Now

I don't know
What to do
To make you love
Like crazy
To make you feel
Just amazingly
Good

I don' know
How to make You
Come'

(YouTube: Ma.Ste. Why Don't You...)

*

'There's no place like home
Wherever you go
There's no place like home
So cosy and warm

You never feel a stranger
In a most peculiar land
For wherever you go
There's no place like home

And Time
And things
And money
You don't give a shit to get
You just let yourself feel at home

It's a perfect place
For Love and joy
The whole planet
And the universe

There's enough for all
No rush
No stress
Enjoy abundance
That's all that you do

And time
And things
And money
You don't give a shit to get
You just let yourself feel at home'

(YouTube: Ma.Ste. Home Everywhere)

*

'I'm gonna hug my lady
Hug my lady tonight
And it's gonna be cool
And it's gonna be so cool

I'm gonna kiss my baby
Kiss my baby alright
And she's gonna be fine
And she's gonna be just fine'

(YouTube: Ma.Ste. Wishful Thinking)

*

'Hurray hurray
I just welcome another day
Is it clouds is it rain
I've got sunshine in my brain

Hurray hurray
Through these dimly waking eyes
You can see
No disguise

How my Soul broadly smiles

Nothing to hide
I've got nothing to lose
In your arms
But my Light
But my dreams
My Heart
My Self
Myself

Waiting on My Lord
To heal all my wounds
Waiting on My Lord
To bring me back to life
Prayers free from words
I'm nothing but grateful

I've been good today
Living like a hermit
Magic magic moments
Of tranquility

I've had no food or drink
Soaking in water
Fire feels so good
They give me strength
They give me faith
When I'm…

Waiting on My Lord
To heal all my wounds
Waiting on My Lord
To bring me back to life
Prayers free from words
I'm nothing but grateful'

(YouTube: Ma.Ste. Open Up)

*

'And I'm almost happy
Here and now
Wanting less
Enjoying peace
Yet longing for wars

Expectations murdered
High hopes killed
No illusions
We are free
Let's surrender to glory and bliss

Time flies
Making lows and highs
Lose their shape
Disintegrate
In this White Light
That surrounds us
And pervades
All that is
Because I AM
always was
and always will be

And I'm almost happy
Here and now
Wanting less
Enjoying peace
Yet longing for wars

Expectations murdered
High hopes killed
No illusions
We are free
Let's surrender to glory and bliss

I wish I had magic spice
To open our eyes
To make us recall
Autumn crocus
To let us focus
On what is our grandest thought
Perfect vision of ourselves
As Who Really We Are'

(YouTube: Ma.Ste. Kashmirian Saffron)

*

'So much Love
Baby
So much Love
Nothing can go wrong
I know you've heard this song
Before

But I can't be wrong
This time
I can't be wrong
We're gonna climb and fly
To meet the sunny days

So give me your hand
And nothing can go wrong
I know we're gonna make it
Before we fall apart

Let's go to the river
Let's swim in crystal clear
To wash away all the fear
I know you're gonna love it
With me

So many roads
The skies are full of stars
We're gonna reach so high
We're never gonna die

So give me your hand
And nothing can go wrong
I know we're gonna make it
Before we fall apart'

(YouTube: Ma.Ste. (For) R.E.A.L.)

*

'Every day
Is voice of Earth and Heaven
Saying
Come
Let's play the game of Life

Your Time
The choice is yours
Though outcome still unclear

There is no penance
Mission
Predestination
What do you want?
I wanna feel Love and joy
I wanna feel
I wanna feel

Light inside
Sunshine
Galaxies of stars

Every morning
You have to start again
To build

Whatever you like
To experience
Here and now

Your Time
The choice is yours
Though outcome still unclear

There is no penance
Mission
Predestination
What do you want?
I wanna feel Love and joy
I wanna feel
I wanna feel

Light inside
Sunshine
Galaxies of stars'

(YouTube: Ma.Ste. Microcosm)

*

'I shall discover the secret
Deep in my Heart
I'll find the Key

As we are all walking questions
How does it work?
Why is it me?

I'll touch and I'll feel
What I've known for so long
It's always been the same
But this time
I want to be
consciously

The wind
It blows my song about
My singing is to heal the world
I start the changes with my own faults
I won't turn away again
Oh no

I stand
The rock it cuts the sky
I raise my hands
The chains let go
The glowing core becomes white-hot
It burns away all my fear
Oh yeah

Pulsating light
In fluttering air
Fire
Vibrating fire

Enough of minor truths
I choose the Golden Rain
In Violet Fire I plunge myself
To blaze with White Light'

(YouTube: Ma.Ste. ... and only like this!)

*

Chapter 31

Closing Passages

I and Maggie are doing the 'consciousness session', also referred to as 'Session of Love'. We are sitting on the floor, embracing each other with our arms and legs, looking into each other's eyes and breathing through our noses. Slowly, regularly, deeply, connecting inhales and the exhales in unbreakable circle.

Time and Space become irrelevant now and here. We are sunk deeply in the lakes of each other's pupils...

'No, The Life Symphony In A Nutshell *is not a good title for Your book. I think you should call it* Bridges...', I can hear Maggie's voice – magic voice in my head. While She's only breathing.
'Jeff Bridges?', I can hardly think, with my high, hyperventilated brain. *'I'll think about it. But first you must tell me who you are...'*
'I am a part of your conscious mind that surrendered to Soul's Light. I am one of the sea snakes swimming across the universe of a quark in your mind. A stream of sub-consciousness. As close to Pure, Unconditional and Everlasting Love as any mind can ever get.'
'You mean a partial illumination? A fragmentary spiritual enlightenment? How can it be possible?'

'Well, apparently, there are still some ties, obstacles, old thinking patterns, you hold on to. And they keep a part of you away from Big Answers. From Ultimate Truths.'
'If you are so close to Soul you must know what it is all about.'

We keep breathing continuously. Enchanted by the regular rhythm of the connected inhales and exhales: in and out, in and out, in and out, in and out, in and out...

'It's about living consciously...', I can hear her whisper in my head.
'But what shall I do to live a better life?'
'It depends on what you want to achieve.'
'And if I want my mind and my body to surrender totally to Pure, Unconditional and Everlasting Love? If I want to become One (a)gain. A re-united, reintegrated being? Master of Being? Pillar of Fire? Burning Bush?'
'Then you have to go to extremes...'
'What do you mean? Isn't my hitherto lifestyle sufficient to get there? With all the conscious breathing, meditations, visualizations, vegetarianism, fasting, "taming" – or rather surrendering to – the elements of Water and Fire, Tibetan rituals, Shiva Kalpa, listening to Aarati, mantras, affirmations, Reiki, Shiatsu, EFT, Feng Shui...'
'No,' She interrupts. *'It's not enough. All that positive thinking and treating spiritual development as just a hobby is not enough. As long as you are so strongly attached to physicality, and all its conditioning, including different relationships; with other people, money, sleep, food and... knowledge, you can only dream about Kingdom of Heaven. And positive thinking is not enough. It's not about philosophy. It's about physiology...'*

'What do you mean?'

'Well, let's take the eating habit as an example. Do you remember all the bliss and bursting with energy you experience in the morning every other Wednesday? After the two days of fasting, during which you sometimes think you are dying. These mornings your pituitary gland (the hypophysis) and your pineal gland (the epiphysis) start waking up and preparing to reset your body to Living on the Light mode (a)gain, according to the genetic codes you inherited through the past generations from those who had not known any food. From before the fall of man. You have these two glands for absorption of natural light, which, together with air from conscious breathing, constitutes the sufficient source of your body energy. And when you start eating again, the glands just go back to sleep...'

'But what about the "middle way"? Do I really I have to stop eating...?'

'You don't have to do anything. You can keep living as a composer, musician, public translator and businessman, dealing with spiritual development only in your spare time. That's your "middle way". That's fine with me. And that's fine with Soul. But if you think about rejuvenation. If you hope for your hair and teeth to grow back, for your complexion to be smooth and shining. If you want to become eagle-eyed, up-straight and daring. If you consider physical immortality, transmutation, transfiguration, dematerialisation and re-materialisation. If you plan to join the Circle of Masters of Being. If this is to be the mission you choose to accomplish through your life... Then I'm sorry, but you must go to extremes.'

'You know in March 1986 in Borki, where I met Maggie, I felt very close to something... To unravelling the Mystery. I hardly slept and ate. Breathing consciously almost 24/7. And the Door in the universe of a quark in my mind was opening slowly letting in more and more of White Light.

And I was walking towards It... But then I saw Maggie's green eyes and long golden hair... And I turned to her light instead... The Door closed... Do you want me now to go back to that Door (a)gain, open it and enter White Light... And if I become fearless. If stop waking up in the middle of the night, horrified by a dream that something bad has happened to my wife, my sons or my aging parents. If I stop worrying so much about life' fragility? Will it mean that I have become less sensitive, less caring...?'
'I don't want you to do anything. But please remember that there are only two kinds of emotions: Pure Unconditional and Everlasting Love, which comes from Heart, from Soul, and all other feelings, which are generated by mind. And it is all up to you which source you choose to drink from Which tree you decide to eat from: Tree of Life or the tree of knowledge of good and evil. It's your life...'

We keep breathing. But I don't think about the breath anymore. The breath is breathing by itself. No more hyperventilation effect. I am filled with White Light. Burning with high and raising flames. I feel only bliss...

'I want you to take over', I declare solemnly.
'OK', She says, *'but then you must forget everything from your past.'*
'Everything?', I ask uncertainly.
'Yes, everything. And I want you to live only here and now', I say to myself.
'Only here and now', myself echoes.

I tighten my embrace. Harder and harder. Until I end up hugging myself.
With tears welling in my eyes, I keep breathing: in and out, in and out, in and out, in and out, in and out... For ever...

*

I am standing on the bottom of Wigry lake, over 70 metres below the surface
of its black waters. I am all glowing with White Light. I raise my clenched fists and jump up. Piercing the darkness. Out of the lake. Into the skies. Now I can see all through the Matrix: the quark structure of the physical dimension is no more a secret to me... And it's not wishful thinking...

*

I'm looking at the PC monitor. My mind is finally empty. I'm going to stop typing now. Just one more statement. It's Time for big changes in my life...

*

GONG!

THE END

Soovowkey, Poland, 12th February, 2009 – 3rd May, 2009

Made in the USA
Charleston, SC
03 June 2011